APR 0 2 2003

T5-AOL-034

DATE DUE	
MAY 0 7 2003	
MAY 1 7 2003	

DEMCO, INC. 38-2931

Modern Middle East Nations
AND THEIR STRATEGIC PLACE IN THE WORLD

OMAN

IRAN
BAHRAIN
QATAR
Persian Gulf
Strait of Hormuz
OMAN
Gulf of Oman
UNITED ARAB EMIRATES
Muscat
Maţraḩ
Sumā'il
Nizwā (Nazwa)
Şūr
SAUDI ARABIA
OMAN
Arabian Sea
YEMEN
N
S
E
W
26°N
24°N
22°N
20°N
18°N
16°N
52°E
54°E
56°E
58°E
60°E
0 50 100 Miles
0 50 100 Kilometers
Albers Conic Equal-Area Projection

Modern Middle East Nations
AND THEIR STRATEGIC PLACE IN THE WORLD

OMAN

TRACY L. BARNETT

MASON CREST PUBLISHERS
PHILADELPHIA

VERNON AREA PUBLIC LIBRARY DISTRICT
LINCOLNSHIRE, ILLINOIS

Produced by OTTN Publishing, Stockton, New Jersey

Mason Crest Publishers
370 Reed Road
Broomall, PA 19008
www.masoncrest.com

Copyright © 2004 by Mason Crest Publishers. All rights reserved.
Printed and bound in the Hashemite Kingdom of Jordan.

First printing

1 3 5 7 9 8 6 4 2

Library of Congress Cataloging-in-Publication Data

Barnett, Tracy.
  Oman / Tracy Barnett.
    p. cm. — (Modern Middle East nations and their strategic place in the world)
  Summary: Discusses the geography, history, economy, government, religion, people, foreign relations, and major cities of Oman.
  Includes bibliographical references and index.
  ISBN 1-59084-517-X
  1. Oman—Juvenile literature.   [1. Oman.]   I. Title. II. Series.
  DS247.O62B37 2003
  953.53—dc21
                                                    2002013007

Acknowledgements

Most of all I would like to thank Mahmoud M. Alhussaini, who dedicated many hours to reviewing these pages and answering my questions. His analysis as a professional person living in the interior of Oman was invaluable to me as I sought to provide a balanced perspective. I hope these pages reflect his desire that his country's story be accurately and fairly represented to the world.

I would also like to acknowledge the contributions of Mohamed El-Tayash, who reviewed the manuscript and helped me particularly with the section on Islam; Sue Hutton, who shared her insights about women in Oman; Äany Brunk, whose insightful and careful copyediting resulted in a better book; and the people of Oman, whose determination to follow their own path with independence and dignity has been an inspiration to me.

Modern Middle East Nations
AND THEIR STRATEGIC PLACE IN THE WORLD

TABLE OF CONTENTS

Introduction 7
  Harvey Sicherman, The Foreign Policy Research Institute

Place in the World 13

The Land 19

History 33

Politics, the Economy, and Religion 57

The People 77

Communities 89

Foreign Relations 99

Chronology 110

Glossary 112

Further Reading 114

Internet Resources 115

Index 116

Modern Middle East Nations
AND THEIR STRATEGIC PLACE IN THE WORLD

ALGERIA
BAHRAIN
DJIBOUTI
EGYPT
IRAN
IRAQ
ISRAEL
JORDAN
KUWAIT
LEBANON
LIBYA
MAURITANIA
MOROCCO
OMAN
THE PALESTINIANS
QATAR
SAUDI ARABIA
SOMALIA
SUDAN
SYRIA
TUNISIA
TURKEY
UNITED ARAB EMIRATES
YEMEN
THE MIDDLE EAST: FACTS AND FIGURES

Dr. Harvey Sicherman, president and director of the Foreign Policy Research Institute, is the author of such books as *America the Vulnerable: Our Military Problems and How to Fix Them* (2002) and *Palestinian Autonomy, Self-Government and Peace* (1993).

Introduction

by Dr. Harvey Sicherman

Situated as it is between Africa, Europe, and the Far East, the Middle East has played a unique role in world history. Often described as the birthplace of religions (notably Judaism, Christianity, and Islam) and the cradle of civilizations (Egypt, Mesopotamia, Persia), this region and its peoples have given humanity some of its most precious possessions. At the same time, the Middle East has had more than its share of conflicts. The area is strewn with the ruins of fortifications and the cemeteries of combatants, not to speak of modern arsenals for war.

Today, more than ever, Americans are aware that events in the Middle East can affect our security and prosperity. The United States has a considerable military, political, and economic presence throughout much of the region. Developments there regularly find their way onto the front pages of our newspapers and the screens of our television sets.

Introduction

Still, it is fair to say that most Middle Eastern countries remain a mystery, their cultures and religions barely known, their peoples and politics confusing and strange. The purpose of this book series is to change that, to educate the reader in the basic facts about the 23 states and many peoples that make up the region. (For our purpose, the Middle East also includes the North African states linked by ethnicity, language, and religion to the Arabs, as well as Somalia and Mauritania, which are African but share the Muslim religion and are members of the Arab League.) A notable feature of the series is the integration of geography, demography, and history; economics and politics; culture and religion. The careful student will learn much that he or she needs to know about ever so important lands.

A few general observations are in order as an introduction to the subject matter.

The first has to do with history and politics. The modern Middle East is full of ancient sites and peoples who trace their lineage and literature to antiquity. Many commentators also attribute the Middle East's political conflicts to grievances and rivalries from the distant past. While history is often invoked, the truth is that the modern Middle East political system dates only from the 1920s and was largely created by the British and the French, the victors of World War I. Such states as Algeria, Iraq, Israel, Jordan, Kuwait, Saudi Arabia, Syria, Turkey, and the United Arab Emirates did not exist before 1914—they became independent between 1920 and 1971. Others, such as Egypt and Iran, were dominated by outside powers until well after World War II. Before 1914, most of the region's states were either controlled by the Turkish-run Ottoman Empire or owed allegiance to the Ottoman sultan. (The sultan was also the caliph or highest religious authority in Islam, in the line of

Introduction

the prophet Muhammad's successors, according to the beliefs of the majority of Muslims known as the Sunni.) It was this imperial Muslim system that was ended by the largely British military victory over the Ottomans in World War I. Few of the leaders who emerged in the wake of this event were happy with the territories they were assigned or the borders, which were often drawn by Europeans. Yet, the system has endured despite many efforts to change it.

The second observation has to do with economics, demography, and natural resources. The Middle Eastern peoples live in a region of often dramatic geographical contrasts: vast parched deserts and high mountains, some with year-round snow; stone-hard volcanic rifts and lush semi-tropical valleys; extremely dry and extremely wet conditions, sometimes separated by only a few miles; large permanent rivers and *wadis*, riverbeds dry as a bone until winter rains send torrents of flood from the mountains to the sea. In ancient times, a very skilled agriculture made the Middle East the breadbasket of the Roman Empire, and its trade carried luxury fabrics, foods, and spices both East and West.

Most recently, however, the Middle East has become more known for a single commodity—oil, which is unevenly distributed and largely concentrated in the Persian Gulf and Arabian Peninsula (although large pockets are also to be found in Algeria, Libya, and other sites). There are also new, potentially lucrative offshore gas fields in the Eastern Mediterranean.

This uneven distribution of wealth has been compounded by demographics. Birth rates are very high, but the countries with the most oil are often lightly populated. Over the last decade, Middle East populations under the age of 20 have grown enormously. How will these young people be educated? Where will they work? The

INTRODUCTION

failure of most governments in the region to give their people skills and jobs (with notable exceptions such as Israel) has also contributed to large out-migrations. Many have gone to Europe; many others work in other Middle Eastern countries, supporting their families from afar.

Another unsettling situation is the heavy pressure both people and industry have put on vital resources. Chronic water shortages plague the region. Air quality, public sanitation, and health services in the big cities are also seriously overburdened. There are solutions to these problems, but they require a cooperative approach that is sorely lacking.

A third important observation is the role of religion in the Middle East. Americans, who take separation of church and state for granted, should know that most countries in the region either proclaim their countries to be Muslim or allow a very large role for that religion in public life. Among those with predominantly Muslim populations, Turkey alone describes itself as secular and prohibits avowedly religious parties in the political system. Lebanon was a Christian-dominated state, and Israel continues to be a Jewish state. While both strongly emphasize secular politics, religion plays an enormous role in culture, daily life, and legislation. It is also important to recall that Islamic law (*Sharia*) permits people to practice Judaism and Christianity in Muslim states but only as *Dhimmi*, protected but very second-class citizens.

Fourth, the American student of the modern Middle East will be impressed by the varieties of one-man, centralized rule, very unlike the workings of Western democracies. There are monarchies, some with traditional methods of consultation for tribal elders and even ordinary citizens, in Saudi Arabia and many Gulf States; kings with limited but still important parliaments (such as in Jordan and

Introduction

Morocco); and military and civilian dictatorships, some (such as Syria) even operating on the hereditary principle (Hafez al Assad's son Bashar succeeded him). Turkey is a practicing democracy, although a special role is given to the military that limits what any government can do. Israel operates the freest democracy, albeit constricted by emergency regulations (such as military censorship) due to the Arab-Israeli conflict.

In conclusion, the MODERN MIDDLE EAST NATIONS series will engage imagination and interest simply because it covers an area of such great importance to the United States. Americans may be relative latecomers to the affairs of this region, but our involvement there will endure. We at the Foreign Policy Research Institute hope that these books will kindle a lifelong interest in the fascinating and significant Middle East.

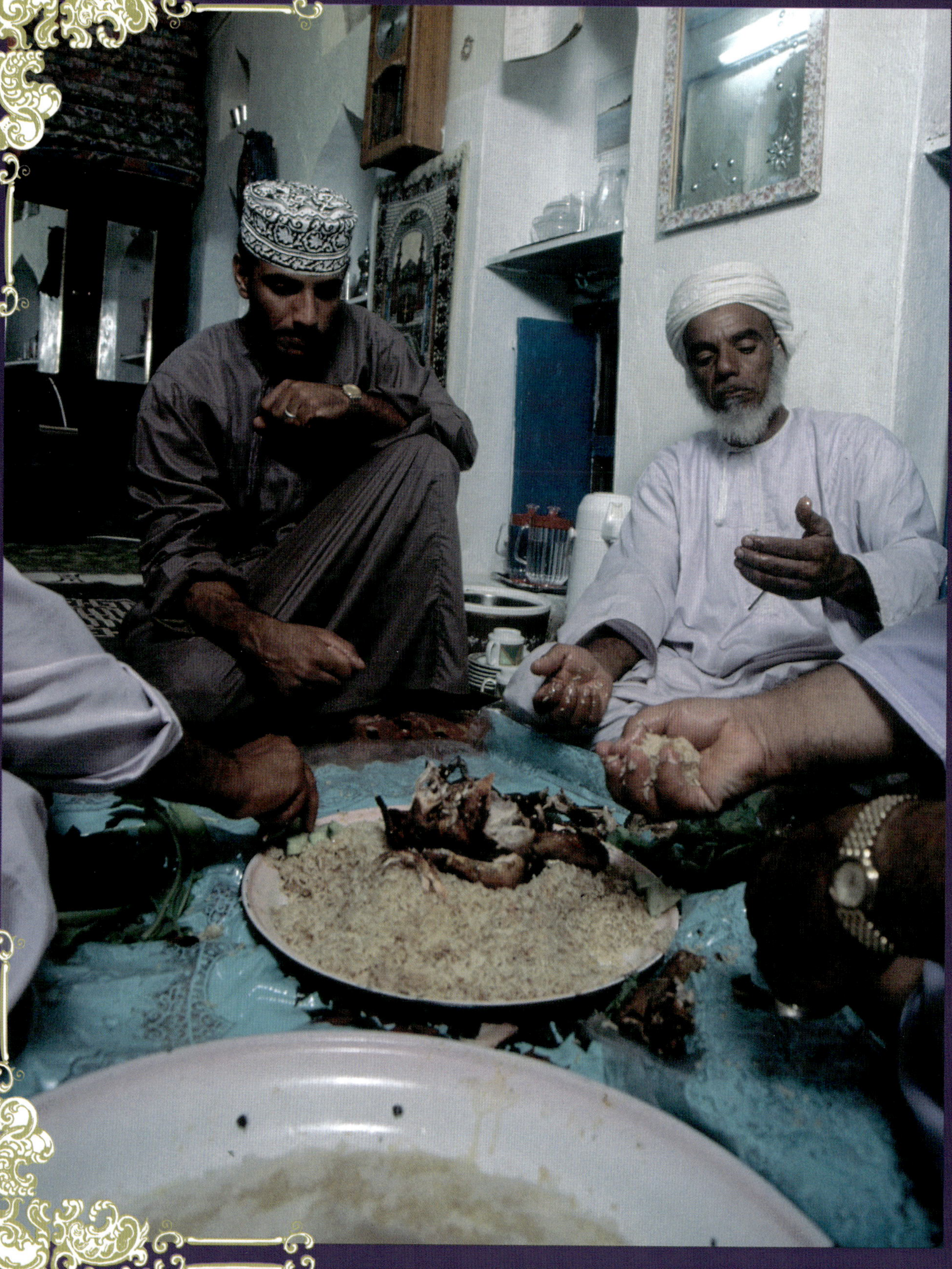

Omani men sit on the floor eating a meal with their hands. For many years Oman was a mysterious part of the Middle East little known to most Westerners; today, however, the country has strengthened its ties with its Arab neighbors and the West, and is emerging as one of the region's most important nations.

Place in the World

Oman—the name conjures images of windswept sand dunes, veiled women and ruthless pirates, dagger-wielding Bedouins and magic-lantern geniis and velvet-robed sultans. It's the home of Sinbad the Sailor and the *Tales of the Arabian Nights*, the legendary land of the frankincense that was delivered to the infant Jesus. Under its sands lies the lost city of Ubar, which has been compared to Atlantis in its majesty and mystery.

But what do we really know of Oman?

For centuries, this country in the southeast corner of Arabia has been as shrouded in mystery as Tibet. Isolated from the rest of Arabia by rugged mountains and the vast Rub' al Khali desert of Saudi Arabia, Oman was as remote and uncharted as the Himalayas.

Oman's history has been distinct from that of other Arab countries. For centuries all that linked Oman to the rest of the Arab world was its Arabic-language traditions and customs, and the peoples' strong belief in Allah. Like the rest of the Arabic-speaking Middle East, the people of Oman are predominantly Islamic. However, most people practice **_Ibadi Islam_**, a form of the religion that is rare outside of Oman. And until the mid-1970s, Omanis were almost completely cut off from contact with the rest of the world through modern conveniences such as telephones, television, and radio. Less than ten miles of paved road existed in the entire country at the time. The vast majority of Omanis did not even have the benefit of a basic elementary school education; only three schools existed in the entire country, and they were only for boys.

Oman's current ruler, Sultan Qaboos bin Said, took over in a palace coup in 1970, a short time after oil was discovered under the country's sands. Since then, Qaboos has undertaken the task of bringing Oman into the 20th century. His government has built schools and hospitals throughout the country, established social programs, and constructed thousands of miles of roads. The sultan appealed to Omanis around the world, many of whom had previously left their country to seek education or a better life, to return to Oman and help with the project of modernizing their nation. Qaboos came to power in the midst of a bitter civil war, and after five years of battle he unified the people under his leadership.

Like many other nations of the Middle East, Oman became important to the Western world when it began to produce oil. In a worldwide economy dependent on petroleum to run the machines of modern industry, Oman's oil reserves, and its strategic location, are vital. Oman's oil reserves aren't nearly as great as those of Saudi Arabia, but the country, with its 1,000 miles (1,600 kilometers) of coastline and its position on the Strait of Hormuz, controls most of the shipping channel through which gulf oil must pass.

Besides oil, Oman is known for its dates—said to be the most delicious in the world. It exports fish from its many miles of ocean

PLACE IN THE WORLD

During the reign of Sultan Qaboos bin Said, Oman has come into closer contact with the rest of the world. Qaboos has worked to improve opportunities for his people by providing an educational system that is among the best in the Arab world, and using the wealth created by Oman's oil reserves to create jobs and infrastructure.

waters, and it has a fairly productive agricultural system, centered around the northern Batinah Coast and the southern province of Dhofar. After years of environmental neglect, thousands of acres have been set aside for nature preserves and once-endangered or extinct species such as the Arabian oryx and **tahr** have been bred in captivity and reintroduced into the wild. And women, whose role under conservative Arab leaders was confined to the home, are now beginning to make a difference in the workplace and in leadership positions in the government.

For a long time Oman has been friendly with the United States and other nations of the West; in 1833 it sent the first Arab diplomatic mission to the United States. The country has resisted involvement in gulf conflicts such as the 1979 Iranian revolution and the Iran-Iraq war of the 1980s. And though **Islamist** rebels in Oman at times have resisted government control, the Qaboos government has brought them under control, mostly through relatively peaceful means.

Oman is far from implementing a democracy—as in most Muslim countries, the head of state is not elected, and the rule of law is heavily influenced by the Qur'an (Koran) and other Islamic texts. There is a tradition of consensual decision-making, as well as a degree of political participation, at the local level. Ibadi Islam is different from other forms of Islam in that it allows for the election of spiritual leaders (called **imams**). However, it should be kept in mind that Oman has never elected a sultan, king, or emir, and that many of the country's 61 imams were not elected, instead inheriting their positions. Also, the election of imams is not open to most of the public: scholars and community elders—all of whom are men—meet for discussions before determining their selection. However, Oman's current government has gradually moved to a more open form of government, and Sultan Qaboos, perhaps the most popular leader in the history of Oman, has indicated that democracy is a long-term goal. As a result, Qaboos has won the allegiance and support of most Omanis.

But things are not perfect in Oman, despite many positive trends. The country still has one of the highest birth rates in the world, and many of its people are still poor. Despite government encouragement, women are still moving very slowly toward taking a greater role in society; nearly two-thirds of Omani women cannot read, and women only contribute about one-sixth of the country's economic activity. Environmental issues will present serious challenges in the years ahead as well. The supply of fresh water, a precious and scarce resource in Oman, will become more important as development increases. And the country now faces what may be its biggest obstacle of all—Oman's oil reserves are expected to run out in within the next two decades. Without the oil revenues that Sultan Qaboos has used to stabilize his country, build Oman's economy, and employ its people, what will happen to Oman in the decades ahead?

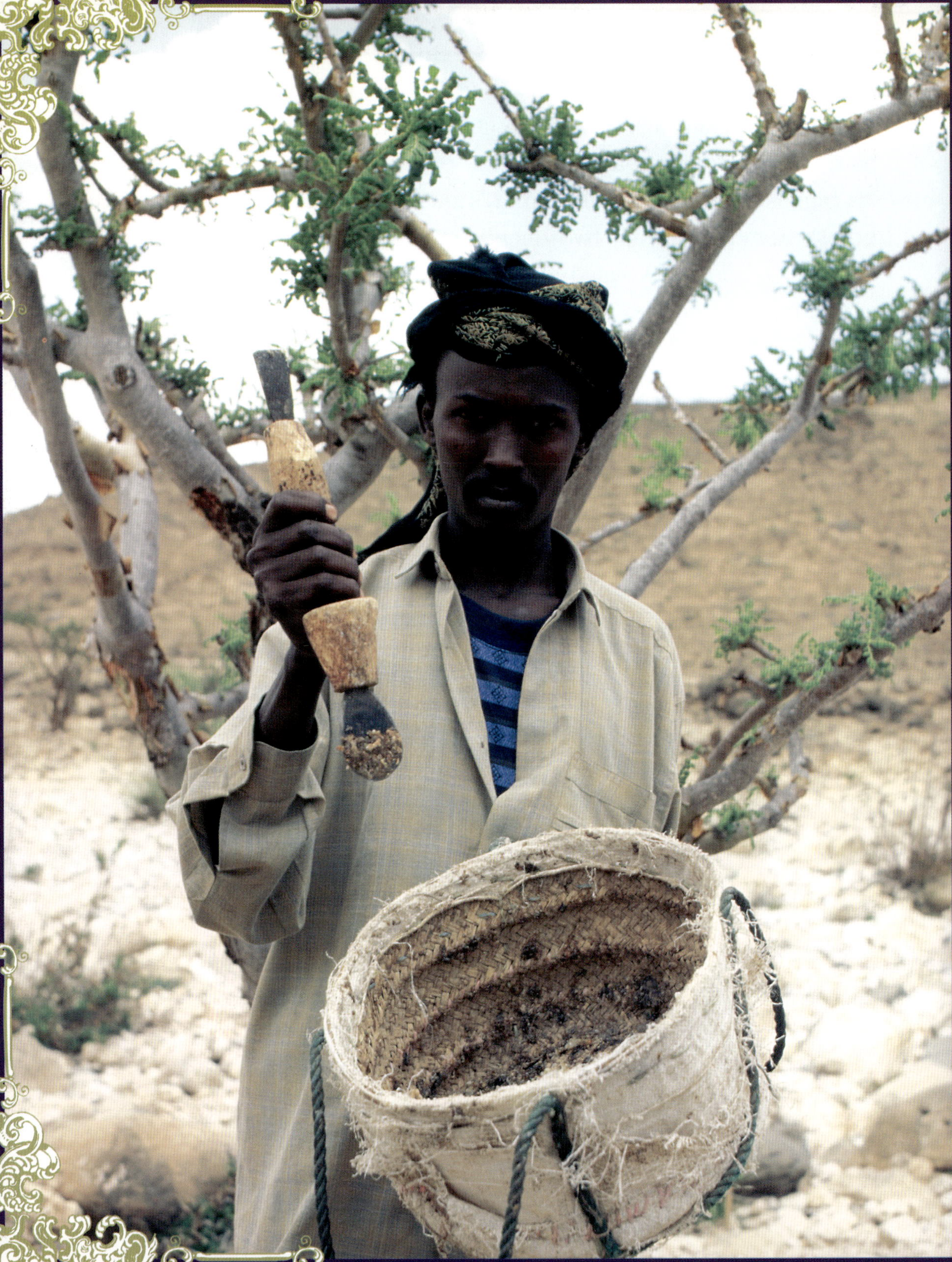

A man collects resin from a frankincense tree in the Dhofar region. One of Oman's earliest civilizations was built around the trade of this aromatic incense, which was used throughout the ancient world for religious and medicinal purposes.

The Land

Oman is a land that has called to curious travelers for centuries, though it's only been in the past four decades that foreigners have been able to travel freely in the country. For all the discomfort one must endure from the furnace-like heat, the scenery is spectacular, the architecture is amazing, and the people, for the most part, are kind and welcoming.

Oman is largely a desert country, but there is much more to Oman than sand and stone. There are no rivers or lakes, but the land is dotted with green, spring-fed **oases**. The capital, Muscat, and the Batinah region receive less than four inches (10 centimeters) of rain per year, mostly during the monsoon season in June, so Omanis have learned to conserve every drop. Over the centuries, the people have developed a complex irrigation system called the **falaj** that carefully shepherds the little rainfall that does occur and channels it to households and farms.

At about 82,000 square miles (about 212,000 sq km), Oman is about the size of Kansas, stood on end. Much of its population of about 2.7 million is concentrated around the ancient capital, Muscat, with its heavy carved gates and its crenellated fortresses.

The country is bounded on the east by about 1,000 miles (1,600 km) of rugged coastlines and sandy beaches. It is amazingly diverse, from the picturesque fishing villages and golden sands of the Batinah Coast in the north to the surprisingly green, tropical southern province of Dhofar. The Hajar Mountains run like a spine parallel to the Batinah Coast in the north, and the ocean of sand known as Arabia's Empty Quarter, the Rub' al Khali desert, connects Oman to Saudi Arabia in the west.

Climate

Oman is one of the hottest countries in the world, with temperatures that can reach 130° Fahrenheit (54° Celsius). A British political agent assigned to Muscat in the early 20th century complained bitterly about the country's heat, describing the hostile conditions extensively in his memoirs:

> Though Muscat itself faces due north, it is surrounded by high cliffs and backs on the rocks, mountains and deserts of the Empty Quarter of Arabia. The effect of this is that the sea breeze which blows in the day is soaked with moisture and produces the maximum wet-bulb temperature, and the land breeze which blows off the red-hot rock and sands at night produces temperatures which I have known to reach 108 degrees at midnight. How one's wretched body stood up against this twelve-hourly change from the maximum wet-bulb to the maximum dry-bulb I have never understood.

It's not always that hot, of course, and those who live there have adapted themselves to the heat and learned to live fairly comfortably. Winters are pleasantly warm; the average annual temperature in Muscat is 84°F (29°C). The Dhofar Region is cooled

THE LAND

Much of Oman is low-lying desert land. In the northeast, the Hajar Mountains run parallel to the Batinah Coast. Smaller groups of mountains run through the Dhofar province in the south of Oman.

by the annual monsoons, which drop up to 30 inches (76 cm) of rain per year on the south side of the mountains. Parts of the Hajar Mountains receive up to 18 inches (46 cm), while Muscat and the Batinah Coast only get about 4 inches (10 cm). Sometimes the monsoons produce flash floods when the **wadis**, or dry riverbeds, become filled with raging water that sweeps away everything in its path. In the interior, severe droughts are common, and summer winds can produce dangerous sandstorms.

REGIONS

Oman can be divided into six main regions, which are very different from each other in terms of both the land and its people: the Batinah Coast, the Hajar Mountains, Inner Oman, Central Oman, Dhofar, and the Musandam Peninsula.

To the north and east of Muscat stretches the Batinah Coast. The **alluvial plain** that stretches between this coast and the Hajar Mountains is the most agriculturally productive region in the country, with date palms that produce some of the plumpest, most luscious dates in the world. A band of palm forest stretches for nearly 200 miles (322 km) along the Batinah Coast. Sometimes the forest is just a few hundred yards wide, while in other areas it spreads to cover nearly half a mile.

A line of oases stretches throughout the plain, watered by the wadis which run down from the mountains to the coast. During rainstorms these can become roaring rivers for a brief time. The region is also irrigated by the channels of the ancient *falaj*.

The other mainstay of the Batinah people is the ocean, where fisherman set off each morning in rafts and dugouts, made of palm bark and wood, and catch fish in large nets or wicker basket traps called *dubai*.

The Hajar Mountain range is quite spectacular, running parallel

A road runs through rugged terrrain in the Hajar Mountains, which parallel Oman's Batinah Coast.

The Geography of Oman

Location: southeast corner of the Arabian Peninsula
Area: about the size of Kansas
   total: 82,031 square miles (212,460 square kilometers)
   land: 82,031 square miles (212,460 square kilometers)
   water: 0 square miles
Borders: Saudi Arabia, 420 miles (676 km); United Arab Emirates, 255 miles (410 km); Yemen, 179 miles (288 km); coastline, 1,299 miles (2,092 km)
Climate: extremely hot and humid along coast; hot, dry desert interior; strong southwest summer monsoon (May to September) in the Dhofar province to the south
Terrain: central desert plain, rugged mountains in north and south
Elevation extremes:
   lowest point: Arabian Sea, 0 feet
   highest point: Jabal Shams (Jabal al-Akhdar), 9,777 feet (2,980 meters)
Natural hazards: Summer winds often whip up huge sand and dust storms in the interior; periodic droughts can be severe

Sources: Oman Ministry of Tourism; CIA World Factbook, 2002

to the Batinah Coast from the northwest to the southeast. The highest point in the country can be found here, the spectacular Jabal al-Akhdar (Green Mountain). Its highest peak, called Jabal Shams, rises to nearly 10,000 feet (about 2,980 meters). The mountains are divided by wadis, which have provided travel routes across the mountains over the ages. The biggest among them is Wadi Sama'il, a valley that forms the major trade route dividing the mountains into the Eastern Hajar and the Western Hajar.

The Hajar Mountain region stretches southward, including the major inland cities of Rustaq in the north and Nizwa in the south. It was the Jawf region of the Western Hajar that formed the core area of ancient Omani civilization. It includes the Buraimi Oasis, a cluster of nine villages that straddle the border with Abu Dhabi and was the scene of a standoff between the Saudis and the British over oil exploration rights during the 1950s. It never turned out to be a major oil-producing area, however.

Inner Oman, together with Central Oman, is generally referred to as "the Interior." Protected from the outer world by the mountains on the north and the vast Rub' al Khali desert to the west, the tribal people of the interior became isolated and inward-looking. To outsiders, the area can seem barren and hostile.

Central Oman, which extends from Inner Oman southward to the Dhofar area, has been described as a sand and gravel wasteland. For centuries it was the realm of a handful of Bedouin tribes. Now, however, oil derricks dot its surface, plumbing its depths for the oil that provides much of the wealth of modern Oman. To the east, between the Hajar and the coast, lie the Wahiba Sands, a range of dune formations.

Off the coast of Central Oman is Masirah Island. Due to its strategic location along a major oil-shipping route, the British located military facilities there from 1932 to 1977, and the United States established a base there in 1980.

Far to the south of the great deserts and mountains of the interior is the Dhofar province. As different from the rest of Oman as the jungles of Peru, Dhofar is lush with tropical greenery. Three clusters of mountains—the Jabal Samhan, the Jabal Qara, and the Jabal Qamar—provide a protective backdrop for a fertile, crescent-shaped plain. The mountains capture the moist currents from the Arabian Sea and the monsoons that sweep through each year, dropping an estimated six inches (15 cm) of rain a year on the coastal plain and up to 30 inches (76 cm) in the mountains.

Dhofar is the home of banana and sugar cane, coconut and cotton. On the drier, north slopes of the mountains grows the scrubby tree known as frankincense. Sap from these trees is dried and formed into incense. Through the ages the rich aroma of frankincense has been used in perfumes and scented religious rituals.

In the early years of Dhofar's civilization, which began about 3000 B.C., fortunes were built by merchants who shipped the incense as far as Mesopotamia (modern-day Iraq), India, and even China. The so-called Incense Coast became wealthy and powerful. Nowadays the Dhofar province's capital city, Salalah (population 300,000), is less a bustling commercial port than a peaceful and pleasant agricultural town, tucked far away from the high-tech commercialism that characterizes the Arabian centers of the oil industry. Dhofar's cool climate, sea breezes, and spectacular mountain backdrop have made it a favorite retreat of the Omani ruling class for generations; in the 20th century several sultans took up residence in the castle of Salalah, retreating from the conflict and poverty that beset their country.

About five miles east of Salalah lie the ruins of the ancient coastal city of Zafar, where 11th- and 12th-century merchants traded the goods they brought from Asia and Africa. Now all that

Oman has a variety of topographical features, including plains, wadis, and mountains.

remains of the great city is an archaeological site, where the casual visitor sees mainly a fenced mound and a collection of rubble.

Not much more exciting to the eye, though perhaps more fascinating to the imagination, is the site of the legendary city of Ubar, which historians have compared to the fabled lost continent of Atlantis or to an Islamic version of the Biblical tale of Sodom and Gomorrah. (See "The Lost City of Ubar," pp. 30–31)

Far away to the north, and isolated even from the northernmost reaches of the Batinah Coast, lies the Musandam Peninsula, also known as Ras al-Jibal. The jagged peaks, which form the northernmost tip of the Hajar range, reach 5,500 feet (1,678 m) at their highest. The eastern border of the United Arab Emirates takes up much of the peninsula and separates the Omani portion of the peninsula from the rest of Oman. Protruding into the strategically important Strait of Hormuz, the area has been occupied by the military and until recently was off-limits to Western travelers. But nowadays, a patient traveler with a week or so to spend can be rewarded with breathtaking views of Scandanavian-style **fjords**

A tranquil inlet of the Musandam Peninsula, also known as Ras al-Jibal. It is an Omani territory, separate from the rest of the country, that protrudes into the Strait of Hormuz.

and picturesque mountain villages, particularly in the rugged Elphinstone Inlet.

Its capital, Khasab, is a small but bustling port. All the other towns in the area, such as Limah, Kumzar, and Bukha, are located on a narrow strip of coast.

Plant and animal life

Despite the desert heat and dryness, Oman is home to an astounding number of wild creatures and plants—and unlike many developing countries, Oman is working hard to protect them. Sultan Qaboos has taken a strong interest in the environment, setting aside a number of nature preserves and implementing a plan for protecting coastal areas. The Sultan loves plants, and in early 1990 a new species of flower was even named after him.

The wildlife of Oman includes several hundred species of birds, lizards, snakes, and scorpions. Several varieties of seashells previously unknown to scientists have been discovered on Omani beaches. Many a traveler has made note, with particular horror, of the camel spider, which can be six inches across!

The delicate Arabian oryx, which was once hunted to extinction in the deserts of Oman, is now an environmental success story. For centuries, great herds of oryx roamed the desert, surviving without water for months at a time and sustaining themselves on the few tiny plants they could find in the desert. A gazelle-like creature with two twisted horns, the oryx is believed to have been the inspiration for the mythical unicorn. Probably one of the spiraled horns made its way to Europe, and the idea of a horned horse became the popular unicorn legend.

For generations the tribal people of the desert hunted the oryx. But with the invention of high-caliber machine guns and military jeeps, killing the animals soon became great sport. During the mid-1900s, caravans of oil-rich princes would amuse themselves by

As these two pictures of Riyam beach (the one on the right taken in 1970, the lower shot in the mid-1990s) illustrate, Oman has undergone many changes. However, while development has proceeded efforts have also been made to protect wildlife and natural resources in Oman.

driving across the desert, killing dozens at a time. By the late 1970s, Oman's native oryx were all gone.

But thanks to the work of wildlife biologists and a number of conservation groups, enough oryx were protected in zoos around the world that the creatures could eventually be reintroduced into the wild. Sultan Qaboos took a great interest in the plight of the oryx and devised a plan, together with the conservation groups, that has resulted in an impressive comeback of the oryx in Oman. A fortunate visitor can even receive permission to visit the sultan's Oryx Farm, where the animals are bred for release into the wild.

The Qaboos government has made great strides in habitat preservation, as well. An area around Ras al-Hadd, the easternmost tip of the Arabian Peninsula, has been protected as a breeding ground for giant sea turtles. Four types of protected sea turtles inhabit the area: the Olive Ridley, the hawksbill, the green turtle, and the loggerhead turtle. All of them come to the shores of Oman from the Indian Ocean each year to lay their eggs.

There is a sanctuary for the Arabian tahr, a type of wild goat, in Jabal Aswad; the tahr nearly became extinct in the 1970s but has come back in large numbers. There is a bird sanctuary in the Dhofar region near Salalah, and a breeding center for endangered species west of the Seeb Airport, where the tahr, striped hyenas, and Arabian wolves and leopards are bred to be reintroduced into the wild.

Some of the world's most productive fisheries are found off the coast of Oman, teeming with tuna, sardines, and other fish that make up one of Oman's biggest exports.

Hardy trees such as the acacia thrive in the desert regions, along with numerous species of wild grasses and thorny bushes. A wide variety of tropical plants can be found in the Dhofar area, from coconut palms to lemons and limes. On the northern, drier side of the mountains in Dhofar are the rare frankincense trees.

The Lost City of Ubar

In the Arab world, the lost city of Ubar is as famous a legend as the story of Atlantis is in the western world. According to legend, Ubar was a wealthy and beautiful trading center in ancient Arabia, from which frankincense was imported throughout the Middle East. However, the people of the city eventually adopted wicked ways; this angered Allah, who caused Ubar to be swallowed by the sands of the desert. There are references to Ubar in the Qur'an (which cites the city's fate as an example of the consequences of a wicked and worldly lifestyle), as well as in the collection of stories known as the *Arabian Nights* and in Bedouin tales passed down by generations of campfire storytellers. The early 20th century British adventurer T. E. Lawrence ("Lawrence of Arabia") called Ubar the "Atlantis of the sands."

Archaeologists thought the city might be more than just a legend, but until the 1990s it could not be found. However, experts used a modern technology known as remote sensing to pinpoint a likely location for the city. The image on the opposite page, which shows southern Oman (the desert area known as Arabia's Empty Quarter, or the Rub' al Khali) was taken by the space shuttle *Endeavour*. The magenta-colored area is a region of large sand dunes. The green areas show rough limestone rocks, which form a rocky desert floor. A major wadi, or dry stream bed, runs across the middle of the image and is shown in white. Ubar is near the wadi, close to the center of the image. The reddish streaks running across the green and white areas are ancient trails leading to and from Ubar. These were used to find the city.

In 1990, archaeological expeditions began searching for the remains of Ubar in the Omani desert. Two years later, in 1992, a large octagonal fortress with thick walls ten feet high and eight tall towers at the corners was discovered. The site may have been inhabited from about 2800 B.C. to A.D. 300. The remains of Greek, Roman, and Syrian pottery—some pieces more than 4,000 years old—were found at the site. These artifacts indicated that the fortress had once been a major trade center, and probably was the fabled city of Ubar.

Interestingly enough, the archaeologists found a large limestone cavern beneath the ancient city. Scientists now believe that Ubar may have been destroyed when a large part of it collapsed into the cavern—disappearing into the desert just as the legends said.

THE LAND 31

This colorful image, taken by a NASA space shuttle, allowed archaeologists to determine the location of a legendary city that disappeared more than 1,600 years ago.

الفرآن ثم ركب اساطير بلاها وخارف جلاها وقال اركبوا فيها بسم الله مجراها
ومرساها ثم نفس نفس المعمين او عباد الله الكرمتن وقال لها انا

This page from a 14th-century Arabic manuscript shows a dhow, a vessel commonly used by Omani sailors in the Indian Ocean. Oman was an ancient trading center, and its sailors were among the most capable in the world.

History

Oman's history stretches back a million years to a time when man's distant ancestors, *homo erectus*, roamed Arabia. Archaeologists have unearthed their rock hand tools, which are estimated to be at least 700,000 years old, in the Dhofar region. About 100,000 years ago, *homo sapiens* migrated out of Africa and across Arabia, displacing their less evolutionarily successful relatives. At that time, Arabia was green and lush, the home of hippopotamus and water buffalo. The nomadic tribes of these times found plenty to eat; they hunted wild cattle, goats, oryxes, and gazelles and roasted them over huge fires. (One archaeologist found remains from 40 settlements in the Rub' al Khali desert of Oman and Saudi Arabia by using satellite maps to find the course of ancient rivers and searching methodically along what would have been their banks.)

Around 20,000 years ago, everything changed dramatically.

Scientists believe the Earth wobbled a bit in its orbit, and that slight movement caused a sweeping global climate change that turned nearly all of Arabia, and much of India, Africa, and Australia, into desert. The lakes and rivers of Arabia dried up, and the winds whipped up ferocious sandstorms and created a sea of dunes. Humans fled northward to find water and to escape the broiling heat. For another ten millennia, there was almost no rain and no sign of human habitation.

Between about 8,000 and 6,000 B.C., the rains returned; with them came the people, and soon Arabia was repopulated. These people who lived in the area that today is Oman are referred to in ancient literature as the **people of 'Ad**. They lived throughout the region from around 4,500 B.C. to A.D. 500.

Among these new arrivals were nomadic herdsmen, whose lives revolved around the cattle they tended. A group of these nomads settled in the Dhofar Mountains, one of the greenest and most fertile parts of Arabia because of the annual visit from the monsoons. Meanwhile, to the north along the Batinah Coast, other ancient dwellers in Oman discovered a rich lode of copper, a metal that was valued for making tools and weapons. The Empire of Magan developed after 2000 B.C. around the mining and trade of copper. Magan was concentrated around what is today the city of Sohar.

It was during this time that frankincense was discovered in the south of Oman. This scrubby little bush is unimpressive—until it is burned. Fire releases from its wood an aroma so sweet that people throughout the centuries have sent its smoke heavenward with the hope that it would be pleasing to their gods. The plant burned with a strange, bright light and was believed to have healing properties. The people of 'Ad learned how to harvest the resin of the tree and dry it on large palm-leaf mats. They built a great city, called Ubar, at the crossroads of the major trade routes of the time, shipping their frankincense as far as Turkey, Greece, India, and China. Ubar

The ruins of Sumhuram are believed to be part of the ancient city of Moscha (called the Abyssopolis by the Roman historian Pliny the Elder). They are located in the Dhofar region of Oman.

thrived on the frankincense trade for centuries. Pliny the Elder, an ancient Roman historian, described the people of 'Ad as "the richest nations in the world." Word spread of the city's riches, and Alexander the Great was planning an expedition to the area when he died in 323 B.C. However, by the fourth century A.D., the city of Ubar had disappeared into the desert. Elsewhere in Oman the incense trade was in decline—in part because of a severe drought and in part because of the rise of Christianity, which did not depend on incense for its rituals.

THE SPREAD OF ISLAM

Muhammad's birth in Mecca in A.D. 570 marked the end of an old era and the beginning of a new one for all of Arabia, including Oman, which accepted the teachings of this prophet during his lifetime. Muhammad's work transformed the region in much the same way that the teachings of Jesus and the development of Christianity transformed the West. By the time of Muhammad's death in 632, there were several hundred thousand Arabs who followed his teachings. This religion became known as Islam. Muhammad's followers spread their beliefs aggressively; within a century of his death, the Islamic faith had spread to southern Europe, North Africa, south-central Asia, and parts of India and China.

By the eighth century, Oman's sea trade was flourishing. The Oman region had a long maritime history because of its strategic location as the link between the Arabian Gulf and the Indian Ocean. Centuries earlier Omani sailors had learned how to best use the **trade winds**, which blow northeast toward India during the winter, then blow the other way in the summer. The Arabs were able to apply their knowledge of mathematics and astronomy to help them find their way across the Indian Ocean. At a time when Europeans were living through their dark ages, and few people traveled more than a handful of miles away from their homes, Arab sailors were exploring the waters far from their home shores. Sohar, in Oman, became perhaps the most important seaport in the Middle East. From the port, Omani ships called dhows carried goods across the Indian Ocean to various ports on the coasts of Africa, India, and even China. The eighth-century voyages of the famous Omani sailor Abu Ubaida bin Abdulla bin al Qassim included a 4,350-mile (7,000 km) trip to the port city of Guangzhou (Canton) on the southeastern coast of China!

Omani sailors and traders also helped to spread the Islamic

The sailing vessel *Sohar* was built in 1981 to recreate the eighth-century voyage of an Omani sailor to China. The dhow was built using traditional methods and equipment in Sur, where dhows are still built today. No nails were used in its construction; the ship's timbers were sewn together with rope. It took eight months for the *Sohar* to reach Guangzhou (Canton).

Oman's most famous maritime figure is Sinbad the Sailor, whose exploits were detailed in the *Arabian Nights*. Sinbad is believed to have lived in the port city of Sohar, although some sources claim that Suwaiq, also in Oman, was the town of his origin.

faith, as well as Arab culture, throughout the region. Along one stretch of African coastline, Omani traders were so influential that by the ninth century a new language, Swahili, had emerged. Swahili combined elements of African (Bantu), Arab, and Persian languages; the people living along this 1,800-mile coastline (modern-day Kenya and Tanzania) developed a culture that was very much influenced by Islam as well as Arab art and architecture.

Omani ship captains took such valued items as frankincense and copper to trade. In return, they acquired ivory, gold, pearls, and **spices**—as well as one other valuable commodity, slaves. The slave trade brought great wealth to Oman. From Oman, African

This 1375 map, which depicts part of Asia and the Middle East (including the Persian Gulf, which is at the bottom) was based on information provided by Arab traders and sailors, as well as from popular travel books of the time and historical references in the Bible and other sources. Kings and other figures are pictured on the map; one of these is the trader Marco Polo and his caravan (upper right) which is heading east to China.

Portugal took control of coastal Oman in the early 16th century, when a large Portuguese fleet and army commanded by Alfonso de Albuquerque conquered Muscat and other important cities.

slaves were sent to other Muslim countries in the Middle East as well as to India.

Arrival of the Portuguese

By the 13th century European merchants like Marco Polo had discovered the silks, spices, jewelry, and other wonderful goods available through trade with the Arabs and the Far East. The Europeans wanted to increase their access to these rich markets. Land routes between Europe and Asia were cut off by the emerging power of the Ottoman Empire, centered in Turkey, during the 15th century, so European countries like Portugal decided to find sea routes to Asia. On a voyage in 1497–99, the Portuguese captain Vasco da Gama sailed around the southern tip of Africa, then northeast into the Indian Ocean. With the aid of an Omani sailor, Gama eventually reached India, where he established a trade agreement with a local ruler before returning home.

Arab merchants resented the arrival of these Europeans, who were cutting them out of the trade profits. Within a few years, Portugal sent its military to protect its ships. A Portuguese force led by Alfonso de Albuquerque sacked Muscat in 1508 and Portugal took control of the city and all the coastal areas of Oman.

The Portuguese did not invest a great deal in Oman. They apparently considered Oman just a way station on the route to their more prosperous holdings in India, and built only the forts that still stand in Muscat and Muttrah. But they controlled the most important coastal areas—Muscat, Sohar, and Qalhat—for more than a century.

The Portuguese conquest led the warring tribes of Oman to lay their differences aside and elect a new imam, Nassir bin Murshid al-Ya'aribi, who set about the task of expelling the foreigners. He led a 25-year campaign to unite the tribes against the Portuguese, recapturing the interior towns of Julfar, Quriyat, Sur, and Ja'alan. In 1643 his forces captured Sohar, leaving the Portuguese in control of only Muscat. In 1645, he signed Oman's first treaty with Great Britain, establishing what was to be a very long and close relationship with that country. Nassir died before he could finish his goal of expelling the Portuguese from Oman, but his successor, Sultan bin Saif al-Ya'aribi, pushed them out of Muscat in 1650.

With the recapture of Muscat, Omanis once more saw an increase in their power and influence in the region. Under the Ya'aribi dynasty, which lasted until the early 1700s, Oman saw its holdings expand to encompass Zanzibar to the south (from where Oman again became a center of the slave trade) and Bahrain in the north. Sultan ibn Saif I implemented a tax on all commerce that went through the Arabian Gulf and used the money to rebuild several towns and to construct a distinctive round fort in his capital at Nizwa.

Establishment of the Al bu Said Dynasty

Three generations of Ya'aribis were considered to be successful and effective rulers, but the coalition of tribes that supported them began to fall apart upon the death of Sultan ibn Saif II in 1718. A 20-year civil war ensued, leaving the country greatly weakened and its influence diminished. In 1738, the Persians (a people who lived in the area that today is Iran) invaded Omani territory and occupied the cities of Muttrah and Muscat. However, Sohar was not taken and its governor, Ahmad bin Said, led the fight against the Persians. Under his leadership the Persians were driven out of the country in 1744.

Ahmad's defeat of the Persians greatly increased his popularity, and he was elected imam, beginning the rule of a dynasty that has continued to rule the country to the present day, with varying degrees of success. (Though he came to power as an imam, Ahmad ruled as **sultan**, a title his descendants also used.) He ruled the country until 1783.

Sayyid Said bin Sultan (1804–1856) was the most effective Omani ruler of the

The fort at Nizwa, famed for its round tower, was constructed in the mid-17th century by Sultan ibn Saif al-Ya'aribi. Nizwa, built at an oasis, today is the largest city in the interior of Oman.

19th century, consolidating his power to extend over much of Arabia and the Persian Gulf and reasserting control over Zanzibar. Sayyid Said bin Sultan was the first Arab ruler to establish friendly ties with the United States, and a treaty with the U.S. was signed on September 21, 1833. The treaty remains in effect, and is one of the oldest treaties the United States holds with any country. When Sayyid Said bin Sultan died, however, the country began a rapid economic decline. To begin with, his two sons divided the country in half, with one son ruling his portion from Zanzibar, the other from Muscat—hence the strange new name of the country, Muscat and Oman, which would stay with the country until 1970. Muscat referred to the coastal areas like Sohar and Qalhat, which were under the control of the sultan. That division led to the alienation of the Omani countryside from the influence of the capital—a separation that would continue until the present monarch, Sultan Qaboos, took control in 1970 and began the difficult process of integrating the two very different cultures of Oman's interior and coastal regions.

Besides the division of the country, another reason for Oman's economic decline was the British decision to discourage the country's slave and gun trades. These had brought a great deal of money to Oman. Great Britain, which had become an extremely influential protector of the sultanate, strongly opposed the slave trade and compelled the sultan to discontinue it. In return, each year the British gave the sultan a large **subsidy** to make up for the lost revenues. This, along with the substantial military protection the British provided, gave them an increasing amount of power in Omani affairs—a situation Oman's sultans resented, but could not do much about.

By the time Sultan Faisal bin Turki came to power in 1888, Oman was in decline. Faisal bin Turki inherited a country that was nearly bankrupt and was beset by warring tribes that had no intention of accepting his authority. The interior of the country, which included almost all of the region apart from the coastal areas and the southern province of Dhofar, was under the control of imams who were chosen by the local tribes. The imams, like their followers, were deeply religious people who felt the sultanate had become corrupted by western influence. These Omanis despised materialism and worldliness, preferring instead to focus on the family, the tribe, and their worship. Their leadership often extended beyond the religious; many imams also served as political and even military leaders, particularly in times of conflict.

In February of 1895, the Sultan's worst fears came true. An army of rebels stormed Muscat and occupied the palace. Faisal and his brother escaped with their lives, reaching the twin fortresses Mirani and Jalali that sit atop stone bluffs on either side of the harbor. There the forces opposed to the sultan kept up a siege for a month, bombarding the palace while the fighting in the streets during that month claimed 150 lives. Finally the British sailed in and restored order. The sultan paid the tribal sheikhs some hefty bribes to go back to their mountain homes, and he reinforced his defenses with better weaponry and a contingent of armed African guards.

Faisal's outlook on the situation did not improve much, however. He was frequently depressed and spent most of his days within the walls of his palace. Eight years later, after a series of rebellions in the coastal port of Sur, the sultan threatened to **abdicate**, or give up the throne, leaving his young son Taimur in charge.

The Mirani fort in Muscat, where Sultan Faisal bin Turki and his supporters withstood a siege in 1895. The fortress had been built by the Portuguese in 1587. Though the arrival of British troops ended the siege and restored order, the sultan's rule remained troubled.

The British persuaded Faisal to stay at the helm of his troubled country. The situation continued to deteriorate, with angry Omanis taking up arms and fighting with the **walis**, or governors, of their regions. British authorities were increasingly alarmed at the number of armed men roaming the countryside and began to push for a halt to the weapons trade. Faisal had reluctantly agreed in 1891 to halt the arms trade, but he badly needed the revenue, so he did not protest the continuing weapon shipments from French arms dealers. The tribal sheikhs were becoming more and more demanding, and the bribes he was forced to pay to maintain order continued to grow.

Violence continued to spread throughout the countryside. In the spring of 1910, tribes in Sohar took up arms against their wali. The sultan traveled to Sohar and paid some more bribes, only to hear about more uprisings in Sur. He traveled from crisis to crisis, trying desperately to restore order. In March 1912, a leading sheikh in the city of Rustaq was assassinated, and the sultan feared that his supporters would be blamed.

Finally the British persuaded the French to stop their shipments of weapons into the country. They offered Faisal an annual **pension** in exchange for an arms control agreement, in which all of Muscat's guns and ammunition would be locked up in a guarded warehouse, and only those with special licenses could be allowed to carry weapons. Faisal feared his subjects would see this as a cowardly surrender of his authority to the British; indeed, many of them did. When he finally agreed to the gun control plan, resentments reached the boiling point. Even the sultan's own brother was rumored to be sympathetic with the rebels. Rebel leaders claimed the sultan had sold his country in return for a pension, and they issued a manifesto stating that Sultan Faisal had failed to enforce Islamic law. Under his rule, they argued, the morals of their country had declined. They accused Faisal of allowing what was prohibited under Islamic law—the sale of tobacco and alcohol—and prohibiting what was permitted, the sale of slaves and guns.

Date-harvesting season was rapidly approaching—ordinarily a time of great peace and celebration throughout the Omani countryside, as the workers in the cities return home to their families to work in the date groves. But unlike previous years, the tensions showed no signs of easing. On the contrary, storekeepers in the souks packed up their wares and sought refuge on ships in the harbor. Faisal desperately sent messages to his British allies, asking for more money to pay to the outraged sheikhs.

The angry sheikhs sent a fiercely worded letter accusing the sultan of treason and threatening to murder any foreigner who stepped into their domain. Two tribes that had warred for generations, the Hinawi and the Ghafri, agreed to join forces in their battle against the Sultan. Their leader, the blind imam Abdulla bin Hamid Alsalmy, was believed to be able to perform miracles. To this day his followers call him Noor A'Dein, the Light of the Religion, and consider him a great leader who rallied the divided countryside into one powerful movement. It continued to gain force, and in the summer of 1913, the most powerful sheikh in the country, Isa bin Saleh, joined them. They moved from town to town throughout the date-producing Samail Valley, eventually besieging the compound where the sultan's son and 60 of his followers were staying.

Faisal paced the palace in a state of agitation, chain-smoking cigarettes and staying up all night, according to palace sources. Sometimes he appeared to be mentally ill. At his wits' end, he wired the British, asking for help. They sailed in with 250 soldiers, and the Sultan's son was released. Faisal died, defeated and humiliated, before the conflict was resolved, however.

PEACE IN OMAN

When Faisal's son took power as Sultan Taimur bin Faisal in

1913, he reluctantly inherited a divided country and a devastated economy. Like his father, Taimur relied on the British for nearly everything: military and financial support, a staff of experts to help him make decisions, and even negotiators for the nearly impossible—but essential—job of winning tribal support.

In the end, it was a kindly and quiet Indian interpreter who worked at the British consul who helped to break the impasse between the sultan and the tribal leaders. In September 1920, a British political agent named Ronald Wingate set out in a dhow for the port town of Sib, where he was to represent the sultan in talks with a group of 30 tribal leaders and some 400 armed soldiers. Wingate was accompanied on the trip by Ehtisham-Ud-Dowlah Khan, his Indian friend and translator. Wingate had been stationed barely a year in Muscat when the job of peacemaker fell to him. The task that awaited him was formidable: the sheikhs did not like the British, and they liked the sultan even less.

Despite the tensions, Wingate's hosts treated him to traditional Arab hospitality. "For two days we talked, squatting on carpets, the sheikhs with their daggers and silver-mounted muskets and Ehtisham and myself drinking interminable cups of coffee, breaking off in the evening for feasting, and continuing again the next morning," Wingate recalled in his memoirs.

Negotiations were going well. The sheikhs agreed to live in peace with the sultan and not interfere with the administration of Muscat or other coastal cities, as long as the sultan agreed to leave them alone. They agreed to pay a duty on exports if the sultan would reduce the fee to 5 percent, which it had been previously. On the third day, however, the two sides reached an impasse. The sheikhs insisted that the agreement should be between the sultan and their imam.

"This was fatal, and I knew I could not possibly agree to it on behalf of the sultan, for this would mean that the sultan acknowledged another ruler," Wingate wrote. "Every argument was used; that there were millions of Moslems for whom their Imam was not Imam; that this was a political, not a religious matter, and so on. But the tribal leaders were adamant."

Wingate was at a loss; the entire agreement seemed headed for the wastebasket. Suddenly, Ehtisham was struck by a brilliant inspiration. He whispered to Wingate in English, "Tell them the story of the Prophet and his negotiations with the people of Mecca!"

Wingate understood immediately. He told the assembled group the story, which they all knew well. The Prophet had negotiated an agreement with the people of Mecca. When it came time to sign the agreement, he presented it as an agreement between the people of Mecca and "Muhammad, the Prophet of God." But the representatives of Mecca saw a problem. If Muhammad were indeed a Prophet of God, they argued, how could he sign an agreement with mere mortals? The Prophet considered the question for a moment and conceded that they were right. So he changed his title to "Muhammad, Son of Abdullah."

Wingate sat back and looked around at the assembled group. They consulted among themselves and then, to his relief, they smiled. The problem was solved. The word "Imam" was simply removed from the document, and everyone was happy.

The Treaty of Sib, as it came to be known, became the ruling document of the country for 35 years. The Muscat government agreed that it would let the Omani tribes alone in exchange for some peace and quiet. But tribal unrest continued in the years after the treaty. **Wahhabi** warriors with the support of the Saudi government continued to wage battles in the name of their own brand of Islam, a stricter and more conservative interpretation of Islam than that practiced by a majority of Omanis, who were Ibadi Muslims. The king of Saudi Arabia, a Wahhabi, expressed a goal of ruling all of the Arabian Peninsula.

Missionaries in Oman

During the rule of Sultan Taimur, American missionaries were allowed to live and work Oman. One of these was Elizabeth Hosman, a young medical doctor from Kentucky who walked with a severe limp but was as strong of character as any Bedouin. Hosman set about the Herculean task of saving the lives—and as she saw it, the souls—of her many patients. The British consul was determined to keep her within the confines of Muscat, denying her permission to travel to the interior on the grounds that it was not safe. But tales of her surgical skills—astounding healing powers in a country where modern medical technology was unheard of—spread from town to town.

Tribal leaders from around the country requested her presence, and she could not refuse them, regardless of the British consul's disapproval, so she asked for help from the American consul in Baghdad, who intervened on her behalf. In 1924, she received permission to travel to Suwaiq and Hazam. There she stayed with a local family and developed a close friendship with several of the women. She performed numerous surgeries and treated a wide variety of patients.

Like other American missionaries to Oman, Dr. Hosman longed to share her views on religion with the Arabs. She was more patient and understanding about their religious convictions than some, such as a missionary named Dr. Harold Storm, who traveled to Dhofar without receiving permission. Dr. Storm expressed great frustration with those who heard his sermons, as he related in his memoirs, *Whither Arabia*:

> The Moslem heart is a heart of stone, and every appeal of Christianity seems to rebound from it without making much, if any, impression. Yet our friendships, our acts of mercy, kindness and helpfulness in hospitals and schools are received with gratitude. Because of these things the missionary is loved, but not Christ. It is this which causes the missionary to Arabia at times to despair of his task.

Taimur bin Faisal didn't like being Sultan, and increasingly did not even seem to care much for Oman, preferring instead to vacation in India. At the time of the landmark Treaty of Sib, he was in India with his Turkish wife, so he wasn't able to attend the signing ceremony. He was depressed about the condition of his country and didn't have the slightest idea what to do about it. He repeatedly expressed a desire to abdicate the throne, but the British wouldn't hear of it. If he was to continue receiving the allowance he needed to support his large family, he had to stay in power, they told him—even if only nominally.

So Taimur put others in charge of the capital and spent most of his time in the peaceful southern province of Dhofar, hiding away in his palace in Salalah, or traveling abroad. British officials like Wingate and the desert adventurer Bertram Thomas were appointed to run state affairs, and they continued to coax the sultan to perform his duties.

A Period of Isolation

By 1930, Sultan Taimur bin Faisal was leaving much of the responsibility of his government in the hands of his son, Said ibn Taimur. Sultan Taimur proposed to turn over the sultanate to his son, and in 1932 he retired to India and left the throne to his 21-year-old son.

The new sultan, the 13th member of the Al bu Said family to rule Oman, was determined to pay off his country's debts and free Oman from its dependence on the British. Despite his youth, he quickly became one of the strictest rulers Oman had ever known. He implemented severe economic policies, virtually halting any kind of development in the country. During his rule (1932–70), Oman slipped further and further outside the currents of modern society.

Unlike his father, Said ibn Taimur did not admire the West for its culture or its technology. He was opposed to education, so he

Members of the Saudi Arabian delegation to the United Nations present their view of the Buraimi dispute in March 1953.

did not permit schools to be built. He prohibited most Omanis from going abroad; those who left were usually not allowed to return, because he feared they would corrupt the values of his kingdom. He didn't even want his people to travel within the sultanate, fearing that it might lead them to conspire against him, so he forbade the coastal residents from traveling to the interior, and those in the interior from going to the coast. He opposed modern technology, such as automobiles and telephones, and he even established a trade agreement with the British that forbade them from importing eyeglasses, books, or radios.

In December of 1955, Sultan Said ibn Taimur received one of the greatest threats to his rule. It had started three years earlier in Buraimi, a cluster of nine villages around an oasis in northeast Oman that straddled the border with Abu Dhabi, part of the United Arab Emirates (UAE). The lure of oil wealth was in the air, several big strikes having been made already in the UAE. Standard Oil of

California was prospecting in Saudi Arabia and expressed an interest in the Buraimi area, suspecting that it might be atop a rich oil deposit. Despite the sultan's absolute opposition to modern technology, he was a practical man, and he knew that more money meant greater independence from British influence. So when Saudi Arabia laid claim to the Buraimi Oasis, both Sultan Said ibn Taimur and the sheikh of Abu Dhabi objected strenuously. Talks began between the Saudi ruler and the British, but they were not able to come to an agreement.

The Saudi king based his claim on Wahhabi influence in the area during the previous century, when the Wahhabis controlled traffic and trade on the desert routes that led through Buraimi. But their influence had faded around 1870, and after that time most Buraimi villagers considered their ruler to be either the sheikh of Abu Dhabi or the sultan of Oman. In 1952, the Saudis began working with officials in Buraimi and in Abu Dhabi to try to persuade them to declare their allegiance to Saudi Arabia. They sent gifts and food and began bribing the local people in an attempt to win their loyalty. According to one account, the brother of the sheikh of Abu Dhabi was offered £20 million to **depose** his brother, take over his country, and turn over all oil rights to the Saudis. He refused, but many others accepted the Saudi bribes.

New York Times reporter James Morris, who accompanied Sultan Said ibn Taimur during 1955 on a historic expedition across the country that ended in Buraimi, noted evidence of the Saudi practice of bribery during his stay in the oasis:

> I sat down for coffee with a group of friendly and eager tribesmen, and one of them, looking as if he had lived all his life on the back of a camel, suddenly reached across and grabbed my wrist. He wanted to see my watch, he said. Was it a Longines? I understood this well-informed interest, for I knew it was the practice of the Saudis to distribute gift watches according to makes: the more important the recipient, the more distinguished

the watchmaker. Thus, since the cases were almost always gold, the best way to size up a man's significance to the Saudi cause was to discover the maker's name.

That same year, before the sultan's expedition, the British had suggested arbitration over the Buraimi border matter, and Saudi Arabia agreed. But only a couple of weeks after the sessions began, the British member resigned in disgust, saying his Saudi counterpart had been involved in the whole affair and had been telling witnesses what to say. The British government issued a sharply worded statement accusing the Saudis of trying to bribe the sheikh's brother to kill him.

On October 26, 1955, the British assigned its military force in Oman, called the Trucial Oman Levies, to take over the Buraimi village Hamasa and evict the Saudis. Colonel Eric Johnson, leader of the Trucial Oman Levies, wanted to conduct the operation nonviolently, if possible; he was concerned that if there were an all-out battle, large numbers of innocent villagers could get caught in the crossfire and killed. Since the number of Saudis occupying the town was relatively small, he thought Hamasa could be captured without firing a shot. He organized a group of women—whom he knew would not be threatened by the Saudi warriors—to go over to their camp and tell the Saudis that they were badly outnumbered and that if they surrendered they would be given permission to leave peacefully. Within hours the conflict was resolved, and all 15 Saudis were awaiting deportation in the back of a pickup truck.

"It was, perhaps, all a storm in a teacup, but it was an early indication, a warning, of the pressures which the possible existence of oil in remote places could bring," wrote noted historian John Bulloch in *The Persian Gulf Unveiled*. "It was the first international dispute in the Gulf area to be caused by the hopes of finding oil, though it was not the last."

But Sultan Said ibn Taimur had grown tired of the business of governing his country, and by 1958, he had virtually shut himself off from the world in his palace at Salalah, Dhofar. Contrary to the strict principles by which he ruled his country, he sent his son, Qaboos, to London to receive a university education.

The currents of world affairs were beginning to penetrate Oman, despite the sultan's efforts. The international Marxist movement found its way to Yemen and from there to Oman, and a group called the Dhofar Liberation Front began fighting for an independent Dhofar. Their guerilla war discouraged oil exploration through such tactics as the explosion of an oil exploration vehicle in 1962. But prospecting continued, albeit cautiously, and in 1964, oil was discovered at Fahud. Oman began exporting oil in 1967. But Sultan Said ibn Taimur still resisted spending the wealth from oil sales to improve his subjects' standard of living; he said it would corrupt them. So the vast majority of Omanis continued to live in poverty and isolation, without education and with minimal health care, until 1970.

A New Sultan, A New Direction

The British finally had had enough of Sultan Said ibn Taimur's reclusive and rigid rule, and they coached and supported his Sandhurst-educated son, Qaboos, who took over control of the government in a non-violent

Sultan Qaboos chats with Great Britain's Queen Mother before a 1982 banquet at Buckingham Palace. Great Britain has had a long association with Oman.

Omanis parade in support of a treaty to demarcate the border between the Republic of Yemen and the Sultinate of Oman in the mid-1990s. The agreement ended a 25-year dispute over the border between the two countries.

palace **coup** on July 23, 1970. Said ibn Taimur went to London, where he died in 1972.

Sultan Qaboos immediately set about the task of bringing his country into the 20th century, using the country's newfound oil revenues to build schools and hospitals, roads and bridges, telephone and water lines, and much more. He appealed to the hundreds of Omani professionals who had left the country during his father's rule so they could pursue an education, asking them to come back and help with the modernization of their homeland.

His campaign was slowed in the beginning by the Dhofar rebellion, which had taken on an international, Cold War dimension. The rebels were receiving aid and military supplies from the Soviet Union (through South Yemen), while Qaboos received a large amount of military and other support from Iran, Great Britain, and the United States. By 1975 the sultan had won over many of the rebels with his amnesty program, which offered to let them return to civil society if they would lay down their arms. Those who would not agree to the amnesty he defeated.

In recent years, with Qaboos as its leader, Oman has perhaps been closer to the west than any other Arab nation. In 1978–79, Qaboos was one of the few Arab leaders to support the Camp David Accords, a peace agreement between Egypt and Israel. He was instrumental in the 1981 founding of the Gulf Cooperation Council (GCC), which has enabled many of the Arab nations of the region to work together on various projects to benefit the area. Sultan Qaboos also became active in the Middle East peace process after the 1993 Oslo Agreement between Israel and the Palestinians. And Omani bases were a key element of the U.S.-led war on terrorism, which began in the fall of 2001.

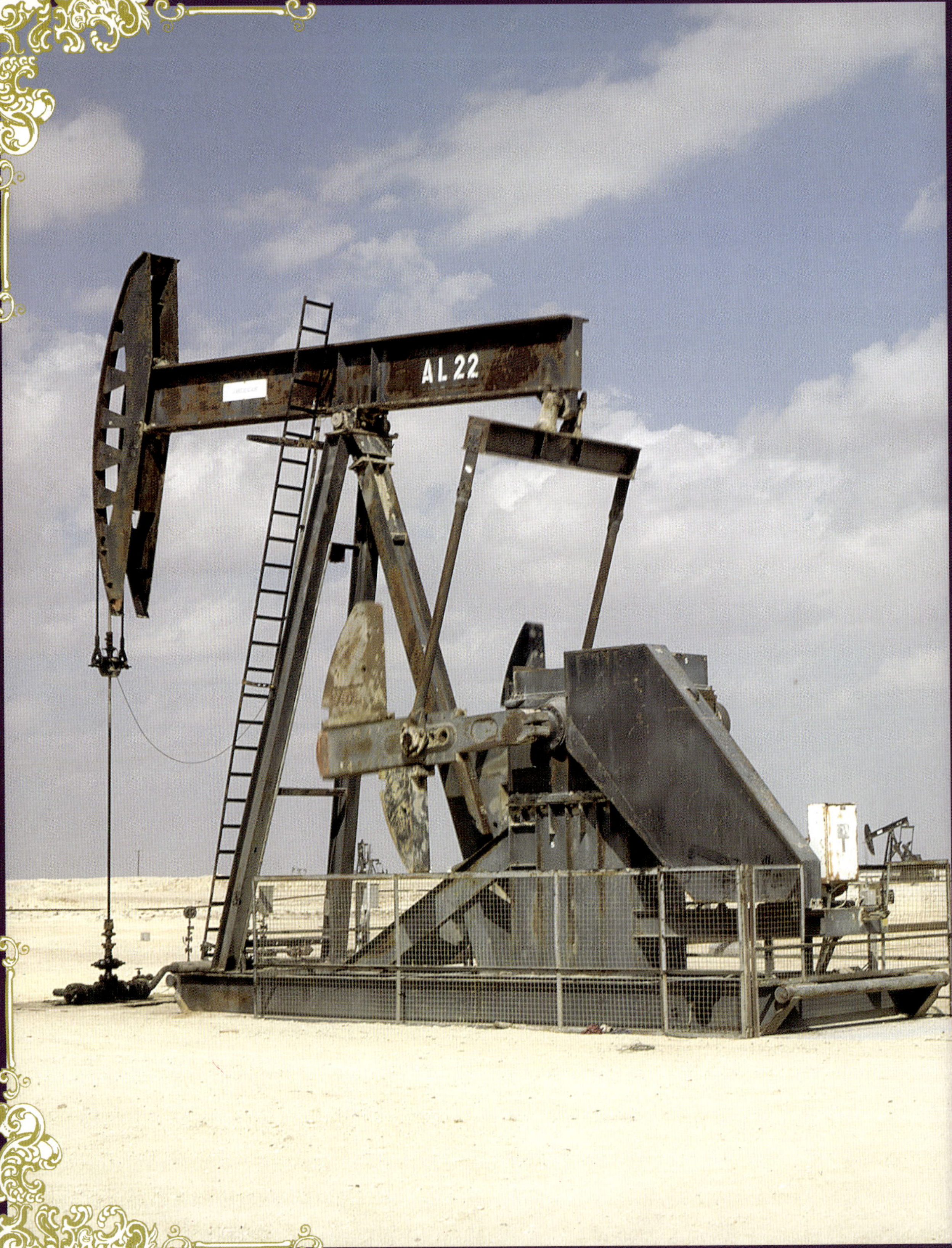
AL 22

Oil is pumped from beneath the sands of Oman. Like Saudi Arabia and the United Arab Emirates, Oman's neighbors on the Arabian Peninsula, oil is the lifeblood of Oman's economy.

Politics, the Economy, and Religion

Modern-day Oman is, above all, a profoundly sensible country. It avoids extremes in religion, never having been caught up in the Islamic fundamentalist movements that have shaken other parts of the Middle East. It is careful with its resources and has chosen a slow, steady, thoughtful approach to economic and community development, avoiding many of the mistakes of its Arab neighbors. Politically, it is a country that looks to a beloved, father-like leader who has been trying to mobilize and modernize people and unify the country.

Oman will be interesting to watch in the years ahead as it implements innovative policies that blend the traditional tribal ways with forward-looking ideas, such as greater participation of women and greater investment in its citizens. After a long period of isolation and neglect that left the country a backward and largely illiterate nation, Oman has had to rely on foreigners to take many professional and leadership positions. Sultan Qaboos has invested millions of oil dollars in the education and training of his people in a process called "Omanization"—a gradual shift of the labor force to be dependent on native Omanis, rather than foreign nationals.

Political system

Oman is one of only two independent countries left in the world that is ruled by a sultan, the traditional leader of an Islamic country. The other is Brunei, on the island of Borneo. Sultan Qaboos bin Said, born of a family that has ruled Oman since the 1700s, has complete authority in the country. The country Qaboos took control of in 1970 was a complete dictatorship. He has gradually moved toward a more open government, reaching out to the people and trying to produce forms of political participation that will translate into support for his modernization plans. It is a very tolerant society by Arab standards; there are no political prisoners in Oman, which is unusual in the region.

Qaboos has a broad range of duties as sultan; he serves as head of state, prime minister, and minister of finance, foreign affairs, and defense. He has a Council of Ministers who assist him in his duties, and a Consultative Council that advises him on social and development policies.

When he began his rule in 1970, Qaboos was at first absorbed with a civil war in the southern region of Dhofar that threatened to tear the country in two. It took five years of battle to reunite the country, and Qaboos himself, who had received military training in Great Britain before becoming sultan, frequently went to the battlefront to rally his troops. But he had inherited a greatly weakened country, and like his father and grandfather before him, he had to rely on the British military to help restore the peace. The

POLITICS, THE ECONOMY, AND RELIGION

The red field in Oman's flag contains the sultinate's emblem, two crossed swords with a khanjar and belt. The flag was created in 1970, and modified in 1995 to make the three horizontal stripes equal in height.

next great task that awaited him was to build the infrastructure necessary to a modern economy, such as roads, phone lines, schools, water and wastewater systems, and power facilities. When Sultan Qaboos took over, there were fewer than ten miles of paved road in the entire country, and the few telephones that existed were concentrated in the hands of a small elite in Muscat.

But by 1982, construction of the modern infrastructure was well underway, and Sultan Qaboos was ready to turn his attention to reform of the political process. The sultan has said many times that his people are not ready for democracy. This is probably true for a number of reasons. For one thing, it will take years for the country to have a fully educated, professional population, because when Qaboos assumed power, there were only three schools in the entire country—two in Muscat and one in Salalah, with a total of 900 students—and they only admitted boys. There were no universities in the country. Within the past three decades, the country has built more than 1,100 new schools, and today girls make up nearly half of the student body.

But the difficulty in establishing a democratic form of government in Oman, and the rest of the Middle East, goes far deeper than a historical lack of public education. It lies in the traditional way that society is structured, as the idea of organized participation in decision-making is a foreign one. This is true at all levels of society, beginning with the makeup of the family. Traditionally, the father of the family is responsible for making all major decisions, and the rest of the family obeys his commands. In the Islamic world, rebellion of son against father or daughter against mother is nearly unheard of. Tribal leaders, or sheikhs, are also generally unchallenged in their authority by tribal members. In the political arena, the idea of a loyal opposition group, such as a competing political party or an advocacy group, simply does not exist.

Oman's unique Ibadi form of Islam, however, does provide a chance for people to meet with their leaders and to complain about perceived injustices. Rulers, from sultan to tribal sheikh, are required to consult with other community leaders in making decisions; if they do not, the people can remove them from office.

Two Omani traditions give people access to their leaders. For the average citizen, there is the **majlis**, an old tribal custom in which the ruler holds regular public hearings, and ordinary citizens can present a complaint or a problem to the ruler. Saudi Arabia and Kuwait still use the *majlis* system. In Oman, Sultan Qaboos no longer holds a formal *majlis*, but he travels around the country in what he calls "meet the people" tours several times a year. Local *walis*, or governors, hold regular *majlis* in each of their states.

The other tribal custom is *shura*, which comes from the Qur'an. In *shura*, rulers sit in consultation with community elders and other notables and exchange views on all the matters of importance of the day. Sultan Qaboos has combined the two principles of *shura* and *majlis* to create the Majlis al-Shura, or Consultative Council. This body is the closest thing Oman has to a legislature. The Consultative Council is only an advisory group to the sultan—Qaboos is not bound to follow its recommendations—but its mem-

Politics, the Economy, and Religion

The sultan is advised by a council of ministers, each member of which heads a different area of government—defense, social affairs, education, transportation, health, and Islamic affairs, for example. Sultan Qaboos established this cabinet in the early 1970s, shortly taking over the reins of government.

bers have considerable influence in the decision-making. The Council looks at all proposed economic and social laws before they are finalized. It also helps create and carry out plans for the country's development. Women have been involved in the country's development plans and policies—several members of the Majlis al-Shura are women, and the government has hired many women as undersecretaries for the Majlis al-Shura, as well as to develop and run social programs.

Qaboos has gone about a very slow and deliberate process in creating the Majlis al-Shura. In 1982 he created the Majlis al-

In Oman, women are permitted to participate in the selection of their representatives in the Majlis al-Shura. Unlike many other countries in the Arab world, Oman's system of government allows a degree of citizen participation; however, power ultimately rests with the sultan.

Dawla, a consultative assembly, to advise him on social, economic, and educational policies. He selected the members of this assembly himself. In 1991, when he felt his people had reached a high enough level of education, he moved a step closer to participatory politics, creating the Majlis al-Shura. Representatives for the Majlis al-Shura were elected from each of Oman's 59 districts, or *wilayets*. In December 1997, Qaboos enlarged the council to 82 members, allowing the larger districts (those with populations of more than 30,000) to have two members. At that time the sultan also decided to allow women to participate in the council.

Selection of the candidates is still a very carefully controlled process. Each candidate must have certain qualifications; he or she must have a good reputation, a good education, and must be at least 30 years old. The selection process is different in each *wilayet*, but for the most part, candidates are selected by a "nominating college" of men and women who are involved in their community. The nominating college then selects two to four top candidates and submits the names to the Majlis al-Shura, which selects the winner or winners from each *wilayet* and passes the names on to the sultan for his final approval.

Qaboos has said that he plans eventually to have the Majlis

Politics, the Economy, and Religion

al-Shura evolve into a full-fledged, democratically elected legislature. He explained his reasoning for this slow, step-by-step process in a 1997 interview with American author Judith Miller:

> In the long run, the Majlis will be elected, yes, by all Omanis. And the Majlis' powers will expand with time, but slowly, so there are no earthquakes. But we are still largely a tribal society, and it's still the government's duty to defend the country. The man in the street often doesn't want or know how to deal with foreign governments or defend the country. He trusts me to do it. That is why these areas have been excluded from the Majlis debate. In this part of the world, giving too much power too fast can be exploited. Elections in many countries mean having the army prevent bloodshed. Is this democracy? Are these happy countries? Do such elections give people real choices? No. They are really just power struggles. I'm against creating such situations when people aren't ready for them.

A constitution, called the Basic Law, was passed in November 1996. The Basic Law was considered revolutionary in many ways. It includes a bill of rights, including freedom of the press, religious tolerance, and equality for women and minorities. It also spells out basic personal freedoms, such as protection from illegal arrest, search, detention, or imprisonment; freedom from torture; and the right of a person who has been arrested to be told immediately the reason for their arrest. It also guarantees that, as in the United States, people are innocent until proven guilty.

The Basic Law codified the idea that Islamic law (*Sharia*) is the law of the land, and that a member of the Al bu Said family will continue to be ruler. Qaboos is a bachelor with no direct heir, so it is unclear who will succeed him. He told Judith Miller that he had already selected two people that could succeed him in case he dies unexpectedly, and he has placed both of their names, in order of preference, in an envelope. But as the Sultan is greatly beloved by his people, it is considered impolite to even discuss the subject.

The court system is based on *Sharia*. As with other aspects of

Islam, there are many versions, and the law practiced in Oman is based, like the rest of Omani Islam, on the Ibadi form.

For misdemeanors, family or personal disputes, and divorce, the cases are generally handled through the *Sharia* court system; for criminal cases, there is a separate magistrate court system; and for business disputes, there is the Authority for the Settlement of Commercial Disputes (the ASCD). There are also separate, specialized boards to handle labor welfare, real estate cases, taxes, and traffic cases.

There are 45 regional *Sharia* courts around the country, each headed by a *qadi*, or judge. The *qadi* bases his decisions on Ibadi *Sharia* law, as well as a series of decrees issued by the sultan on matters not covered by *Sharia* law. Courts are open to the public. Parties may have an attorney represent them, but it is not required. The cases are handled quickly. The *Sharia* judge questions all of the parties involved; attorneys are not generally allowed to cross-examine the witnesses, as they do in American courts, although attorneys, plaintiffs, and defendants may submit questions to the judges, and some judges may decide to allow the attorneys to ask the witnesses questions. The judge usually issues his decision immediately after the trial.

Judges are extensively trained in *Sharia* law at the Institute of *Sharia* Jurisprudence, Counsel, and Guidance. The government has sent many of them abroad to receive masters' degrees in *Sharia* sciences.

Criminal cases are handled by criminal court in the capital or the four magistrate courts in Salalah, Nizwah, Sohar, and Sur. Misdemeanors are punishable by fines of up to 500 **rials** (about $190) or imprisonment from ten days to three years. A criminal investigation is conducted by the Royal Oman Police, and the police bring their evidence before the court. As with the *Sharia* courts, a defendant may have an attorney if he or she is wealthy enough to afford one; but for those who can't afford an attorney, the government does not provide him with one, as in the United States. During the trial, the defendant and his attorney, if he has one, must stand in a metal enclosure. The trial generally goes quickly; a twenty-minute murder trial, for example, is not unusual. If a person disagrees with a sentence, he or she may appeal the decision to the criminal court in the capital. The criminal court's decisions are final, but if a person feels that he has still not been treated fairly, he or she may make an informal appeal to the state advisor for penal affairs, or even to the sultan himself.

Economy

Before oil was discovered in 1967, Oman's tiny economy was based mostly on farming, fishing, and boat making. With the discovery of oil and natural gas, the economy grew rapidly and Oman quickly became dependent on its petroleum revenues; by the mid-1990s, these revenues were nearly half of the country's **gross domestic product**, or **GDP** (the total value of all the goods and services a country produces in a year) and oil made up about 82 percent of Oman's exports. But since the country's oil reserves are expected to run out sometime in the next 16 to 20 years, the government has been working very hard to diversify its economy—that is, to develop a wide variety of revenue sources, so it won't have to be dependent on just one.

Another challenge the government faces is unemployment. Currently the unemployment level hovers around 5 percent, but brighter prospects for Omanis have led to bigger dreams, bigger incomes, and much bigger families. The children of a sizeable baby boom are now coming of age—44 percent of Oman's population was under the age of 15 in the year 2000—so large numbers of young people will be entering the work force in the years ahead. Sultan Qaboos is well aware that if the well-educated younger generation is not given job opportunities, its members will be easy targets for the Islamic fundamentalist movements that have incited unrest in other Middle Eastern countries.

At the heart of the government's economic plan is the concept of "Omanization"—that is, gradually lessening its reliance on foreign workers and replacing them with educated Omanis. To that end, the government has invested heavily in its people by building more than 1,000 schools and a public university. At least three private universities are scheduled to open soon. Each one is linked with prominent British universities. The British have expanded their traditional relationship with Oman into the educational field, working closely with the government to set high educational standards and carry out educational reforms.

The Economy of Oman

Gross domestic product (GDP*): $21.5 billion
GDP per capita: $7,923
Inflation: 1 percent
Natural resources: petroleum, copper, asbestos, some marble, limestone, chromium, gypsum, natural gas
Agriculture (3% of GDP): dates, limes, bananas, alfalfa, vegetables; camels, cattle; fish
Industry (40% of GDP): crude oil production and refining, natural gas production, construction, cement, copper
Services (57% of GDP): government, tourism, banking, information services
Foreign trade:
    Imports—$5.4 billion—machinery and transport equipment, manufactured goods, food, livestock, lubricants
    Exports—$10.9 billion—petroleum, reexports, fish, metals, textiles
Currency exchange rate: 0.3845 Omani rials = $1 US (fixed rate)

*GDP, or gross domestic product, is the total value of goods and services produced in a country annually. All figures 2001 estimates. Sources: World Bank; CIA World Factbook, 2002.

Politics, the Economy, and Religion

Traders check prices on the big board at the Muscat Securities Market, Oman's stock exchange, which was established in 1990.

Another keystone of the economic plan is ***privatization***—a necessity in a country that relies on the oil industry for 80 percent of its government funding. Oman has tried to persuade foreign corporations to invest in its tiny economy, and despite the skepticism of naysayers, has been remarkably successful. In 2000 the country joined the World Trade Organization, opening doors for more foreign investment. In 2001, for example, the country opened the world's most efficient container port in Salalah. With more than $300 million in investments by the shipping giant Maersk Sealand and some $130 million from the Oman government, the port is managed by a private-public partnership—an example of just the type of relationship that the government is pursuing.

Another problem with relying on the oil industry is that it employs few local people. Despite the fact that it represents nearly half of the economy, it only employs 2 percent of Oman's workforce. Another problem is the environmental impact of the industry; Oman's white sand beaches have been despoiled by oil slicks more than once. Oil tankers that pass through the gulf have been known to flush their tanks and empty their oily wastes into the waters, contaminating the beaches and killing fish and birds. Local officials have fought with oil companies and neighboring countries to increase punishment for illegal dumping, but it's hard to catch the offenders because they usually do it at night.

The second-largest sector of the economy, after petroleum, is the services industry. This includes tourism, which has become increasingly popular since Oman has been opened to the world. Its palm-lined, white sand beaches, its ancient ruins, its colorful local culture, and its vast deserts attract a variety of travelers who are looking for a change of pace. The country is working hard to preserve its natural environment, its culture, and its archaeological sites so that tourism will continue to be a growing source of revenue in the years ahead.

From the beginning, the sultan's task of modernizing, growing, and diversifying his nation's economy has been a challenging one. He implemented a series of five-year plans, beginning in 1976. The first, which coincided with the oil sector boom, aimed to establish the infrastructure for a modern industrial country: government buildings, power stations, and communication centers. The second,

Fishing boats arrive with their catch at dawn in Muscat. Before the discovery of oil, fishing was a staple of Oman's economy.

POLITICS, THE ECONOMY, AND RELIGION

Oman has been successful in attracting and developing industries in the country. A series of five-year plans have helped broaden the economy into areas other than oil, although petroleum remains the largest segment of Oman's economy.

which covered the period from 1981–85, tried to complete the infrastructure with projects that were needed to modernize the economy and improve people's lives in the countryside (for example, improved irrigation systems). The third, from 1986 to 1990, attempted to move development plans further along, but a sharp drop in worldwide oil prices forced the government to scale back its plans.

The fourth plan, which covered the period from 1991–95, focused on the dual process of economic diversification and Omanization. By the end of 1995, only 36 percent of the total workforce were Omanis, leaving the country heavily reliant on foreigners. The goal was to bring that number to 42 percent by the year

2000. The fifth plan, covering 1996–2000, called for more participation from the public and from the private sector. It employed sophisticated computer modeling techniques to plan Oman's development in the context of regional and global trends. Oman's current five-year plan is supposed to continue the previous plan, paying particular attention to the development of gas-related industries, tourism, agriculture, fisheries, and financial services.

During the 1980s, as part of plans to diversify the economy, Qaboos invested in the country's agriculture through programs such as land distribution, subsidized loans to buy machinery, and advice on modern irrigation methods. But attempts to expand the country's agriculture have met with some problems. Chief among them is the lack of water in the desert country. Modern irrigation led farmers to pump water out of the underground water table faster than the scant rains could replenish it, and saltwater from the sea began to seep in. A problem known as saltwater intrusion began to develop (this is common in other seaside agricultural

To distribute water throughout Oman, the ancient *falaj*, a system of canals that capture rainwater from the mountains and channel it to homes and farms, has been repaired and upgraded. Some parts of the *falaj* are thousands of years old.

areas, such as California, as well). Some coastal residents of Oman began drawing salty water in their wells, and the brackish irrigation water has killed mango trees and vegetable gardens in the Batinah coastal region to the north.

The government responded to the problem by creating a Ministry of Water Resources in 1990, which launched a series of measures that would help the country care for this precious resource. For example, they put a temporary halt on the drilling of new wells; built recharge dams to hold the rainwater in the wadis long enough for it to seep back into the ground, thus replenishing underground aquifers; and began the massive project of repairing the ancient *falaj*. This innovative underground irrigation system has been the country's circulatory system, carrying mountain rainwater and cold, clear spring water to the people of the desert like human veins carry nutrients through blood to the cells. Unfortunately the *falaj* has been a recurring military target beginning with the Portuguese invaders in the 16th century. So although some 50 percent of the country's water needs were still provided by the *falaj*, by 1990 an upgrade of the system could provide even more.

With an eye toward the future, Omanis are now investing in Internet technology, infrastructure, and training. In 2002, Oman led all the Arab countries—including Egypt, Lebanon, and Saudi Arabia—in growth of Internet bandwidth. The country is laying the groundwork to become a major hub for Internet-based commerce in the region by courting international fiber optic and satellite companies.

Religion

The people of Oman are unpretentious, deeply spiritual, egalitarian, and anti-materialistic. To them, the first duty is to God, whom they call Allah; their second duty is to their family. Duty to community, career, and country come afterward.

Omanis were among the first to accept the teachings of the Prophet Muhammad (570–632). These teachings are the basis of the religion called Islam. The word Islam comes from the Arabic verb *aslama*, which means roughly to gain peace by submitting to the will of Allah.

When Muhammad was 40 years old, he began receiving revelations about the oneness of Allah and the folly of worshipping idols. These revelations are written in the Qu'ran, the sacred text of Islam. The Qu'ran teaches Muslims, or followers of Islam, how to conduct their daily life in all ways, from diet to divorce laws.

Muslims believe Allah is supreme, and that Muhammad was Allah's last prophet on Earth; he followed other prophets such as Jesus, Moses, and Abraham. Islam is based on five basic precepts: *shahadah*, a profession of faith that there is no God but Allah, and that Muhammad is the messenger of God; *salat*, a prayer performed five times a day, always facing the holy city of Mecca; *zakat*, a charitable donation to those less fortunate; *sawm*, fasting from dawn to dusk during the month of Ramadan (the ninth month of the *Hijri*, or Islamic calendar); and *hajj*, the pilgrimage to Mecca that Muslims are encouraged to make during their lifetimes.

Muslims worship in buildings called mosques. Some are quite simple, but many are characterized by beautifully ornate Arabic architecture. Most include a minaret, a tower from which a *muezzin* cries out the call to prayer five times a day in a haunting, melodic chant.

After the death of Muhammad, Islam split into several sects. The two major divisions are between the Sunni Muslims and Shi'a Muslims. The split between these two groups arose from a dispute over who would succeed Muhammad after his death. His only heir was his daughter, Fatimah; she was not eligible to succeed him because she was a woman. Most followers supported the decision of an assembly of Muhammad's advisors, which selected a man

The enormous Sultan Qaboos Grand Mosque, completed in May 2001, can hold up to 20,000 worshippers. An institute of Islamic studies is located nearby.

named Abu Bakr as the first **caliph** (God's representative on earth). Although Abu Bakr was a close friend of Muhammad (and the father of the prophet's second wife), he was not related by blood. This indicated that the Islamic leader would be selected by the strength of his faith, not because he was descended from Muhammad.

A smaller group of followers disagreed. They believed that the caliph should be chosen from Muhammad's descendants, and felt that Fatimah's husband Ali, who was also Muhammad's cousin, was the rightful successor. Ali was eventually elected as the fourth caliph in 656; he was murdered in 661. When Ali's son was not chosen to succeed him as caliph, his followers, calling themselves Shiites, broke away from the rest of the faith.

Sunni Muslims make up the largest percentage of Muslims

worldwide. Of the total Muslim population today, more than 80 percent are Sunnis while Shiites account for about 15 percent. In Oman, however, the proportions are much different. About 22 percent of the Muslims are Sunni, while less than 3 percent are Shi'a. The great majority—about 75 percent of Oman's Muslim population—follow a variant form of Islam called Ibadi.

Ibadi Islam

The Ibadi are members of an Islamic sect that today exists mainly in Oman, East Africa, the Mzab valley of Algeria, the Nafus mountains of Libya, and the island of Jerba in Tunisia. Ibadi Islam developed from the Kharijis, originally followers of Muhammad's cousin Ali who seceded from the group of his supporters (hence the name Khariji, which in Arabic means "seceders") in the seventh century. The Khariji were strict adherents to the prophet's teachings. They regarded Muslims who differed with their views as rebels against the faith, and killed them.

By the eighth century, the Khariji began to moderate their position. The killing of other Muslims was discouraged. The most influential Khariji imam at this time was Abd Allah ibn Ibad. His followers—who became known as Ibadis—founded communities in parts of Africa and southern Arabia; they also became the leaders of Oman, where Ibadi Islam remains the state religion.

The Khariji, and Ibadis, believed that Muslims should follow the person best qualified to lead. That person was chosen by the men of the community, based on his ability to uphold Islamic law. If the group decided a leader was unqualified, he could be removed. This tradition led to a basic sense that any man, regardless of his social class, could become an imam.

The notion of the imam in Ibadi Islam is unique. On one hand, it agrees with Sunni beliefs by discarding the criteria of heredity in succession; on the other hand, it elevates the religious and spiritual role of the imam in the way the Ja'afari Shi'a do. The last true imam to unite the entire country of Oman under his power was Ahmad ibn Said, who ruled from 1744 to 1783. He founded the Al bu Said dynasty that remains in power today; however, he and his descendants rejected the title of imam for that of sultan. Unlike an imam, the sultan's position is hereditary; the sultan also is considered a secular, rather than spiritual, leader. Throughout Oman's history, this has resulted in tension between the sultanate (followers of the sultan) and the imamate (those who preferred to follow their imam). Typically the rule of the imam has dominated in the rugged desert region of Oman's interior, while the coastal regions tended to adapt more readily to leadership by the sultan—although Qaboos has been successful in working closely with both populations to achieve national unity.

Ibadism is a more moderate form of Islam than that found in some countries of the Middle East. While there have been some radical fundamentalist groups that have tried to launch movements in Oman over the years, they haven't gotten very far—perhaps because of the moderate nature of the Omani character, derived from Ibadi Islam. Ibadis prefer simplicity, and avoid some of the elaborate embellishments that have evolved in some other forms of Islam. Their mosques tend to be less ornate, and their services do not include music. But their non-materialistic style, which can be considered strict or severe by some non-Ibadis, has not carried over into a fanatic or judgmental approach with others.

The country has a tradition of religious tolerance; in the past American and British missionaries have been allowed to set up practices in the country. Sultan Qaboos himself has set aside land for Christian churches and Hindu temples, although they are mostly for the foreign nationals who come to live in Oman. Most native Omanis are more than satisfied with their long-held Islamic traditions.

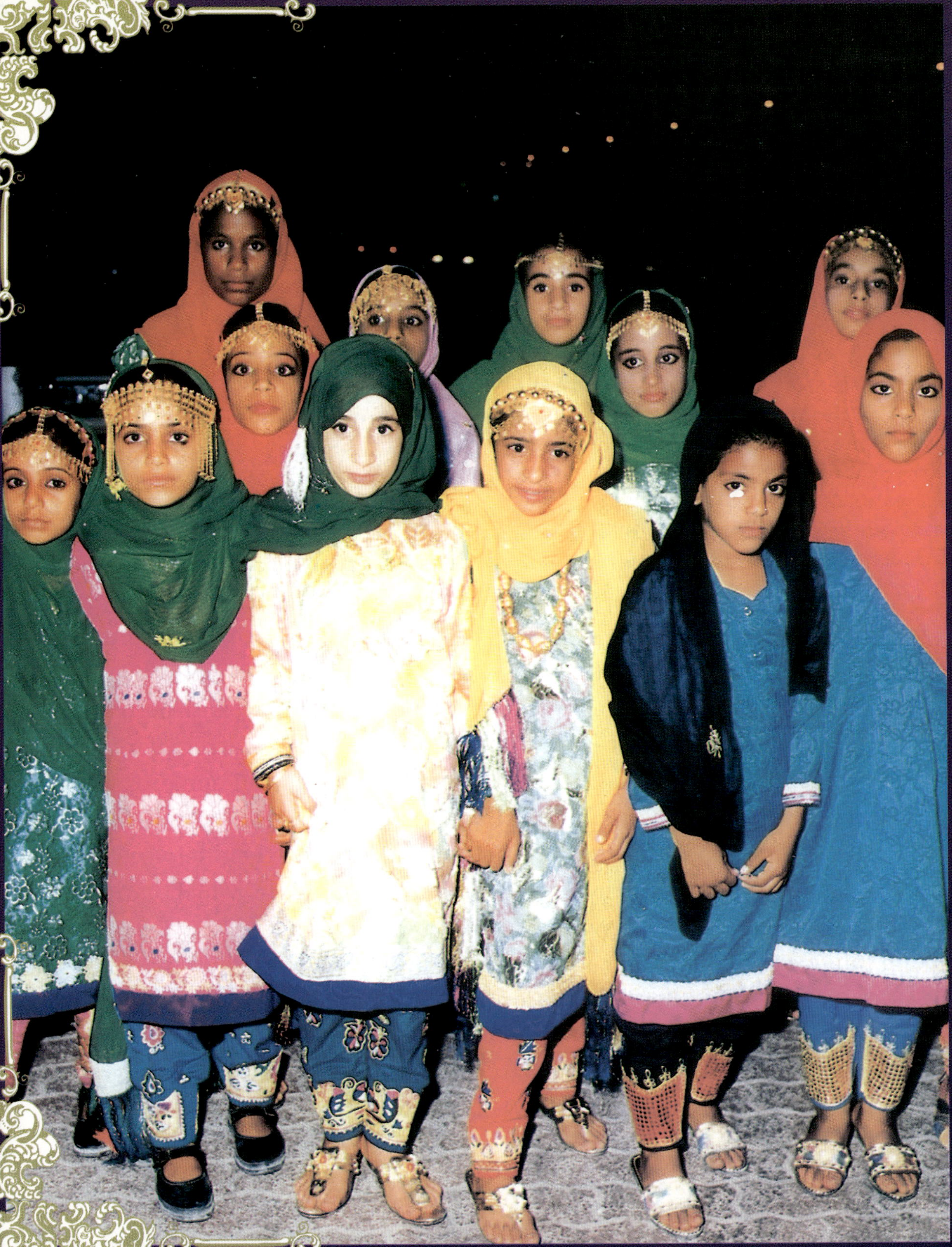

A group of Omani schoolgirls wearing traditional garb. Historically, the culture of Oman was influenced by outsiders because of its location on the major trade routes; however, Oman is first and foremost an Arab country where Islam is practiced by nearly 90 percent of the population.

The People

Western travelers most often are drawn to Oman because of its burgeoning economy, or, increasingly, its spectacular scenery and ancient ruins. But perhaps a better reason might be to meet its people. Omanis have been known throughout the ages for their graciousness, their hospitality, and their sense of loyalty and equity. They can be equally fierce in battle, and when a matter of honor is at stake, they have fought to the death.

The Omanis have a rich and diverse heritage, colorful traditions, a savory cuisine, and a gracious aspect that shows the best of Arab hospitality. Because of their cautious and conservative nature, and a commitment to the environment and to the people, they have been able to retain much of their heritage while incorporating the best of what modern society has to offer. In this way, they have managed to avoid many of the problems that are typical of rapidly developing countries:

high crime rates, widespread pollution, destruction of family and community, and loss of cultural traditions.

The country's position on major shipping routes for most of its history has opened it to a diverse population. Of the country's estimated 2.7 million people, 80 percent are native Arab Omanis. The remainder are foreign nationals with a wide variety of backgrounds: Indian, African, Persian, and Baluchi, to name a few. Baluchis, who come from the Makran coast of Iran and Pakistan, tend to live in the Batinah Coast area and in the capital. Many of them serve in the military, and others work as day laborers in the port towns. Many of the Africans who live in Oman are descendents of slaves; others are immigrants from Zanzibar, an island off the coast of East Africa that was once under Omani control and has retained close ties with the country. There are also many Indian Omanis, in part because of the long history of commerce between the two nations.

As with most countries, there are regional and ethnic differences. But nearly all Omanis share the common bond of Islam. They are devout Muslims, like other Arabs, but they subscribe to a more tolerant interpretation of Islam with regard to the treatment of women, who in most parts of the country are not as strictly segregated from the men as in the rest

Arabian horses were mentioned in ancient writings, and throughout history Omanis have been known as proud horsemen. Thoroughbred horses are raced throughout the year in Oman; horses are also decked out with colorful ornaments and ridden in parades.

of Arabia, and the **burkha**, or veil, is optional in most parts of the country.

Oman's women, spectacularly clad in the most colorful costumes in Arabia, wear a short tunic-style dress similar to the Indian *salwar*, with loose-fitting pants underneath. Some women, particularly the Bedouin, wear a heavy black robe that covers everything but the hands—but even the robed women wear spectacularly colorful clothing underneath. The head is always covered, whether by a robe or a simple colorful cloth. Many women enhance their already dramatic eyes with **kohl**, a black eyeliner kept in a special silver container.

In some parts of the country, women wear a particularly unusual type of *burkha* that takes the form of an elaborate mask. This mask only covers certain parts of the face, usually the cheeks, forehead, and nose, and protrudes in a beak-like shape around the nose. The black mask is frequently tinged with colorful, sparkly hues. It is meant to do two things: enhance a woman's beauty, while demonstrating her modesty. Most Westerners unaccustomed to the mask remark on its appearance with alarm or distaste. Anthropologist Unni Wikan, who lived for six months in the north-

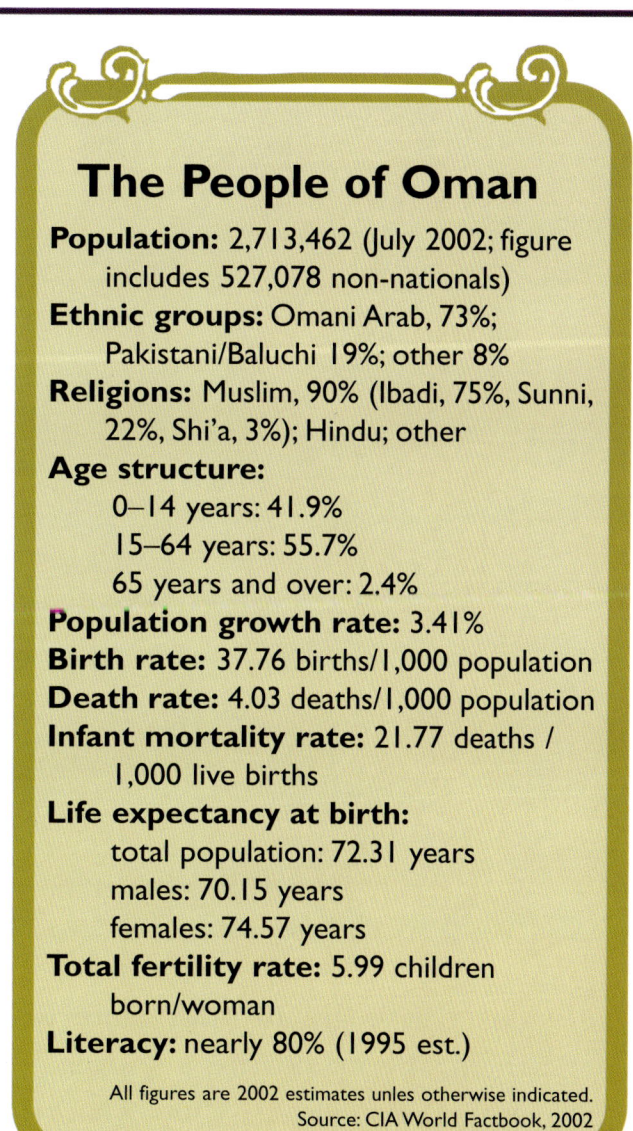

The People of Oman

Population: 2,713,462 (July 2002; figure includes 527,078 non-nationals)
Ethnic groups: Omani Arab, 73%; Pakistani/Baluchi 19%; other 8%
Religions: Muslim, 90% (Ibadi, 75%, Sunni, 22%, Shi'a, 3%); Hindu; other
Age structure:
 0–14 years: 41.9%
 15–64 years: 55.7%
 65 years and over: 2.4%
Population growth rate: 3.41%
Birth rate: 37.76 births/1,000 population
Death rate: 4.03 deaths/1,000 population
Infant mortality rate: 21.77 deaths / 1,000 live births
Life expectancy at birth:
 total population: 72.31 years
 males: 70.15 years
 females: 74.57 years
Total fertility rate: 5.99 children born/woman
Literacy: nearly 80% (1995 est.)

All figures are 2002 estimates unles otherwise indicated.
Source: CIA World Factbook, 2002

This map shows the distribution of population in Oman. The Batinah Coast, with its many fishing villages, and the Dhofar region in the south contain the largest clusters of population, although the remaining people are spread fairly evenly throughout Oman. The Bedouin, who make up a small part of Oman's population, mostly inhabit the desert interior of the country.

ern coastal town of Sohar studying the women's culture during the 1970s, wrote that it took some time before could understand the beauty of the devices; but with time, she assured, one can begin to appreciate them. As for the women who wear them, the masks are a source of great pride, Wikan reported; generally, she wrote, they wear them because they prefer to, not because they must.

The men's clothing is less colorful but just as dramatic. A long, brilliant white robe called a **dishdasha** is fairly universal, sometimes with a belt of silver or leather. The head is covered, sometimes with a turban, sometimes with an elaborately embroidered cap, and less frequently with a traditional Arab head cloth and a black goat-leather circlet around the crown of the head. In the countryside and villages, men tend to carry a rifle and wear the traditional **khanjar**, a curved sword in an intricately decorated silver sheath.

THE PEOPLE

GENDER ROLES IN OMAN

There has been some progress in terms of the woman's role in Oman, with Sultan Qaboos an advocate of women's rights. But change comes slowly, and as with the rest of the Arab world, the man remains king, in the home as in politics.

In the rural areas and smaller villages there is still a traditional tendency to segregate the sexes. In many homes there are separate living spaces for the women and children. The men mostly socialize together, and women are not active in the workplace. They still maintain the traditional role of home and family, for the most part. However, in the more urban areas and particularly on the coast,

An Omani family makes use of a small boat to cross Wadi Shab, an oasis near Sur.

women are joining the workforce in increasingly larger numbers. They have been encouraged in this regard by the Qaboos administration, which recognizes that the country needs the participation of all its citizens and is trying to involve women in the Omanization process. Also, younger couples are more likely to have adopted less rigid gender roles than their parents.

The statistics show that despite its best efforts, Oman still has a long way to go: A 2002 study found that only 16 percent of females are in the workforce, compared to 84 percent of men. By comparison, 31 percent of women work in the United Arab Emirates and 60 percent in the United States. However, Oman has a higher rate than such Arab neighbors as Saudi Arabia (7 percent) and Yemen (an abysmal 2 percent).

Women are not as far behind the men in terms of education, considering the starting point 30 years ago. Girls at this point are expected to receive an average of 8.5 years of education, compared to 9.6 for boys (that compares to 11.2 and 10.3, respectively, in the UAE, and 16.4 and 15.5 in the United States).

Most Omanis are ethnic Arabs, but the country's population includes people originally from South Asian countries like India, Pakistan, Sri Lanka, and Bangladesh, as well as from Africa.

Silver jewelry, including the traditional *khanjar* dagger and incense burners, are on display in a shop in Muscat.

Art, Architecture, and Culture

The artisanship of Omanis is breathtaking, with master silversmiths, goldsmiths, and coppersmiths who labor over intricate pieces of jewelry, decorative weaponry, and other pieces that differ little from the work of their ancestors of antiquity. There are artisans of many types, but particularly well-known are the silversmiths, whose *khanjars*, *kohl* boxes, and coffeepots are frequently sought by international travelers. There are also many excellent potters, weavers, and woodcarvers, whose work reflects the Omani love of beauty and geometric design.

Most local commerce is conducted at the *souk*, or market, where one can go to buy the traditional curved *khanjar* and its silver sheath, or a flowing white *dishdasha* to wear for a visit with locals.

Halwa, an Omani candy, is traditionally served as a symbol of hospitality. A cook stirs the halwa mixture, which include eggs, starch, sugar, and other ingredients, in a *mirjal* (large pot) for at least two hours.

Halwa is usually served before coffee in Omani households.

These outdoor markets, where turbaned vendors sit cross-legged on the ground to hawk their wares, can lose a visitor in their depths. There visitors can find an ornate two-foot-high coffee pot, or a silver cylindrical prayer holder, or an antique gunpowder horn. The tourist fortunate enough to speak Arabic can sit in a teahouse with the old men and listen to stories about the pirates and the Portuguese of days long gone by. And one who is very lucky indeed might spot a glimpse of some colorfully clad Omani women, most of whom keep to themselves and don't mix with foreigners.

Omanis, like other Arabs, are known for their centuries-old architecture, with its graceful and geometric lines, its large inner courtyards, and its wind towers and open spaces designed to catch the lightest breeze.

Everyday Life in Oman

Life is much different on the coast than in the interior. Nowadays fishermen use outboard motors on their wooden, canoe-shaped crafts, but life's rhythms are still very much like they have been for hundreds of years. Coastal fishermen rise at dawn to net mackerel, sardines, and tuna. The Indian Ocean off the coast of Oman contains one of the richest fisheries in the world. The fish are still dried the old-fashioned way, spread out over acres of blazing sands along the beach.

Along the Batinah coastal region, the farmers who raise the bulk of the country's food can be found; the women, too, work the fields and tend the animals, and the villages dot the green wadis and the golden shores. For generations, the people have cultivated the date palms that grow in a verdant belt along the coast. When the British first began colonizing the area, they often had a hard time finding the workers they needed during harvest season, as city-dwellers

A farmer plows a field in the Al Jabar region of the Al Akhdar Mountains. Despite the sultinate's large oil revenues, traditional farming methods are still used.

Using traditional methods, a potter and a weaver practice their craft in Oman.

would migrate to the date groves to be with their families for the date harvest.

In the desert regions of the interior, the people water their fields and gardens using the ancient *falaj* irrigation system. The people of the interior are in general more traditional, more religious, and less influenced by the West. The culture is influenced by the Bedouin, the tribal, nomadic people who once dominated the area. They are an introspective people, made generous by the need to share when food and supplies are scarce, and made strong by the extreme heat and drought they must endure.

The Bedouin are now a relatively small minority group in Oman. There are still an estimated 500,000 living throughout the Arabian Peninsula, but many have abandoned their traditional ways with their tents and their camels and other animals. "[T]oday, a Bedouin camp of the 'traditional' kind is as rare in Arabia as the oryx," wrote historian John Bulloch. "Like the oryx, the Bedouin is 'preserved' in a few places, or has found a habitat in which something akin to the old life is possible. From a distance, the settlement may even look as it used to do, with the black tents, the children tumbling about, and the camels and the sheep and the goats. But in the tent there will be a radio or two, often a television set with the aerial topping the roof-cloth, oil lamps or even electricity from a portable generator, and a store of tinned food and a few cases of 'Pepsi' or one of the other ubiquitous drinks beloved of the sweet-toothed Arabs."

Some live in their camps outside the city limits; others set up their camps far from civilization. Most have houses in the cities now, where the women and children stay. And the men have come to rely on pickup trucks to transport their sheep and other animals to new pastures, rather than moving slowly across the desert with their families in tow.

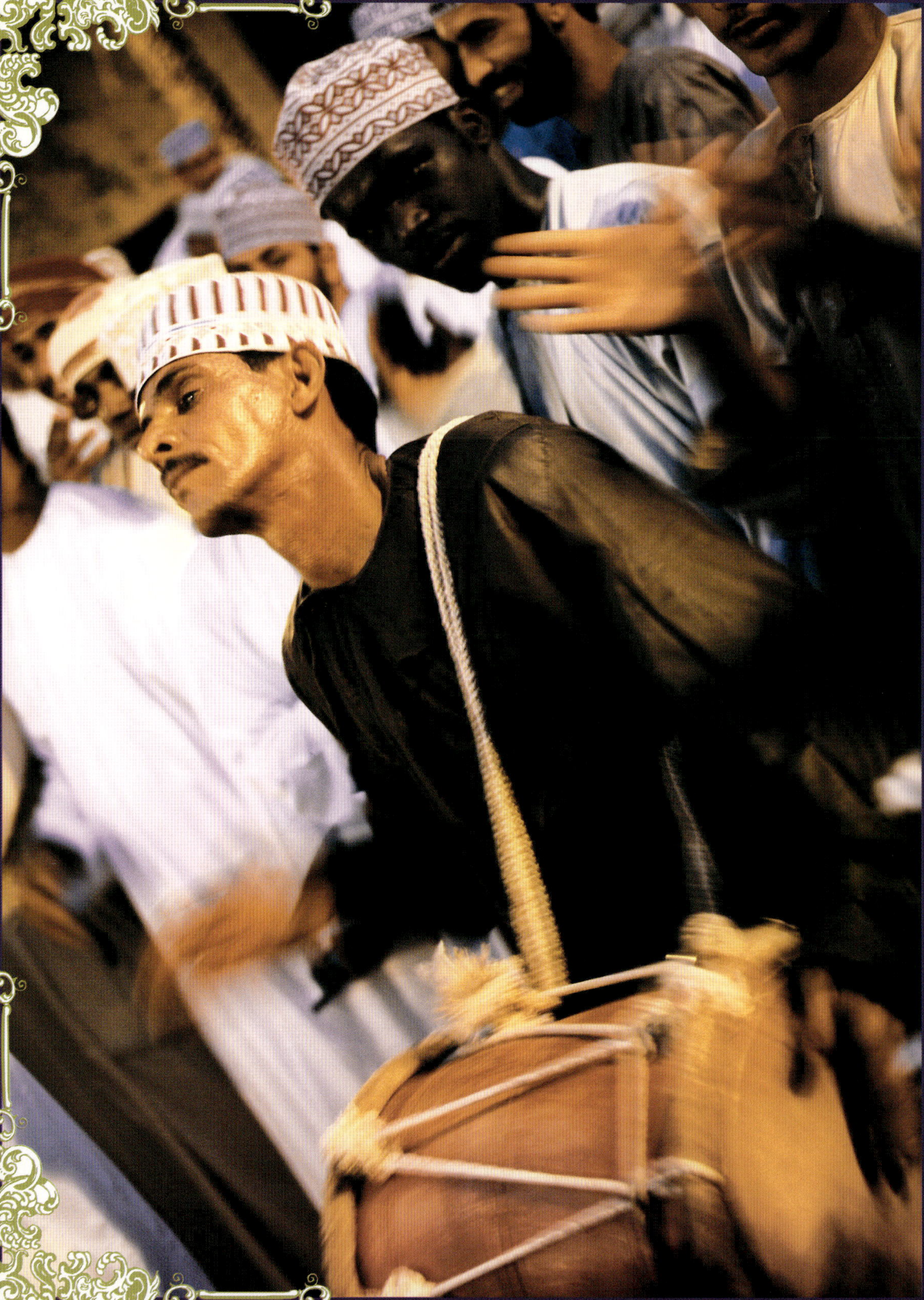

An Omani drummer plays music at a dance in Qurayyat.

Communities

A tour through Oman is in many ways a voyage through history; this splendid little kingdom has managed to combine the best of a wide range of traditions with the best of modern society. The fishing villages of the Batinah Coast in the north are a world apart from the desert-surrounded cities of the interior, and Muscat, with its 21st century conveniences and its ceaseless drive to lead the country forward, is as different from the peaceful southern port of Salalah as one could imagine.

The communities of Oman can be divided into six main categories: first, the people of Muscat and its sister city Mutrah, together with the other major coastal cities, Sur and Sohar; second, the people of the Batinah Coast, who combine fishing and agriculture as their livelihood; third, the inland cultivators of cities like Rustaq and Nizwa, who have for centuries eked a living from the desert soils; fourth, the Bedu or Bedouin tribal people, who live in the desert plains of the south and west; fifth, the people of the tropical province of Dhofar, who in some ways are more similar to the people of Yemen and East Africa than their northern countrymen; and sixth, the mountain people of the Musandam Peninsula, known as the Shihuh.

Muscat

Two enormous medieval fortresses, Mirani and Jalali, are the first thing a visitor sees, sitting high atop the enormous rock bluffs at the city's gates and guarding it like sentinels. Unlike many Arabian cities, where towering skyscrapers of concrete and steel have replaced cottages of palm and stone, the old port town of Muscat still enchants travelers with its ancient feel. You can still find ancient labyrinths of narrow streets, and fisherman plying the miles of abundant fisheries in their wooden or palm-bark dhows.

Leading from the ancient walled area of Muscat is the beautiful palm-lined avenue that locals affectionately refer to as "the Corniche." Another area is Muttrah, home of a winding labyrinth of streets that lead an explorer to the souk.

Muscat, which was founded some 2,000 years ago, hasn't always been Oman's capital. In the olden days it was a small and unimpressive town compared to the likes of Sohar, which lay a day's camel ride up the Batinah coast (today, of course, visitors can take a bus or a Land Rover up the coastal highway and arrive in less than three hours).

Sohar and the Batinah Coast

Sohar was believed to be the home port of Sinbad the Sailor, whose fictional exploits have made their way into nearly every American schoolchild's library. A thousand years ago, the city was the largest in the nation and attracted commerce from as far away as China. Archaeologists believe the city dates back to at least the

Buildings in Muttrah have a distinctive look.

third century B.C. Sohar was sacked twice by invading armies during its colorful history, and until recently it was just a shadow of its former self. But under the Qaboos administration, a Sohar Development Corporation was created and the city began to thrive. Now Sohar has twice won the title "Best Arabic City," and is highly rated for its beauty and liveability.

But all of the towns of the Batinah Coast, as the coastal region that stretches to the north and west of Muscat is called, have their own special charm.

Traveling northward along the coast, there's the village of Sib, where British agent Ronald Wingate reached his historic accord in 1920 with the tribal sheikhs on behalf of the absent Sultan Taimur bin Faisal. Historically, the city-dwellers of Muscat have escaped to Sib to take respite in its green date groves from the heat waves of summer.

Further north is the village of Barka, home of an impressive fort and an even more impressive tale from 18th-century Omani history. It was here that Ahmad bin Said, father of the Al bu Said

These photos illustrate the changes that have taken place in Oman since Sultan Qaboos's reign began in 1970. Both show Ruwi, which has grown from a sleepy village (in the left photo, which was taken in the 1960s) into Oman's commercial hub (in a 1995 photo, below).

dynasty, played out a legendary dinner party ruse that finally rid his country of the brutal occupying Persian armies in 1744. Six years after the Persian invasion, Ahmad invited Persian leaders to a huge gathering and a feast at Barka, to celebrate a treaty in which the Persians had agreed to withdraw from Sohar. As they sat down to enjoy the meal, a drum was sounded and, according to the legend, a crier announced to the Omani villagers: "Anyone who has a grudge against the Persians may now take their revenge." Only a handful of Persians survived the ensuing massacre.

Further up the coast is the village of Suwaiq, where U.S. missionary Dr. Elizabeth Hosman spent a memorable day in 1924 treating a "streamlet of needy humanity," including an important sheikh, who lay in a nearby date-palm hut burning with fever. Hosman succeeded in healing the suffering young man and earned the undying gratitude of that village. Later she learned that this young sheikh was the only leader who had been able to keep the peace among the tribes of that region.

Further down the coast from Muscat is Sur. This ancient city is said to be the original home of the Phoenicians, who developed an alphabet on which all others in the West, including ours, are based. Sur has developed into a modern coastal city that, like Muscat, has retained much of its medieval character. Its pristine beaches provide respite from the oppressive heat, and its fortresses still stand guard, reminders of its days gone by as the world's most powerful center of the slave and gun-running trades. Sur is also home to a still functioning dhow builders' yard, where at any time a dozen dhows might be in the works.

INTERIOR

Nizwa, the major city of the interior, was the capital of the imams, who did not give their allegiance to the Sultan unless they felt he deserved it—and for some periods of Omani history they did not, so Nizwa served as the center for the Imam Wars. Its reputation, deserved or not, as a violently conservative Islamic city was one that struck fear into the hearts of **infidels** (a term for nonbelievers). Some nineteenth century British explorers reportedly lost their heads—literally—for disguising themselves in the garb of Bedouins for the purpose of penetrating the interior of Oman. One who dared was Wilfred Thesiger, who donned Bedouin robes to explore the Omani countryside by camel. He was denied entry to Nizwa—and unlike other prohibitions, he chose to heed this one. Others who visited without such tricks, like Bertram Thomas, were welcomed and treated with the coffee and conversation customary of Arab hospitality. Some historians think the hostile tribesmen were reacting more to the intruders' deceptiveness than to their status as Christians or Westerners.

The most impressive structure in Nizwa is the distinctive round tower-like fort, which was built in the early 1600s by Imam bin Saif al-Ya'aribi as a defense against the Portuguese. It was a common practice in those days to throw unwanted prisoners from the top of the tower, according to legend—but some Omanis doubt this legend. Bin Saif al-Ya'aribi later became sultan and led the campaign that finally drove the Portuguese out of Oman.

Nowadays Nizwa is known for its artisans and its **halwa**, a delectable candy made of *ghee* (a type of butter), starch, brown sugar, cardamom, and honey.

Rustaq is another of the interior's major cities and has played a major role in the country's history. Rustaq served for a time as the capital of the interior.

Bahlah, another town of the interior, takes its name from the ancient tribe of the Bahila. Bahlah has a reputation for being a center for witchcraft and black magic, and the home of the evil **djinn**, or geniis. Perhaps the reason for this reputation is a collection of fascinating geological formations that lie near Bahlah, including a mysterious white mountain known locally as "Witch Mountain." It's not hard to imagine the stealthy djinn living in the white mountain, which gleams in the sunlight, contrasting strangely with the surrounding grey, black, and red hills. Geologists call these types of formations "exotics" because they don't blend in with the surroundings. The formations at Bahlah comprise the largest collection of exotics in the world.

COMMUNITIES

DHOFAR REGION

A visitor to the lush, green landscape of Dhofar would think he or she had stepped into another land, far from the desert sands of Arabia. The summer monsoons wash this region with welcome rain each year, leaving Dhofar cool, wet, and green for much of the year. Culturally and geographically speaking, Dhofar has more in common with East Africa and neighboring Yemen than it does with the Omanis on the other side of the Dhofar mountain range. But despite a history of rebellions and uprisings in Dhofar, a strong bond has also existed with Muscat to the north. Traditionally, the sultan has maintained a palace in the Dhofari capital city, Salalah, and Sultan Said and Sultan Taimur spent a great deal of time there. Nowadays the bonds are even stronger, as Sultan Qaboos is half Dhofari.

Dhofar's history goes back at least to the days of the frankincense trade, which was believed to be centered in the ancient city

Commercial buildings in Muscat. The names of businesses are printed in both Arabic, the official language of Oman, and English.

> The frankincense delivered to the Baby Jesus at his birth was said to have been from the Dhofar region of Oman. The other gifts brought by the three kings were myrrh, an aromatic gum used for medicinal purposes, and gold. At the time, gold was considered the least valuable of the three!

of Ubar. Salalah and other Dhofari port towns shipped the precious incense throughout the East and as far West as Rome to be used in religious ceremonies, until the rise of Christianity caused a rapid decline in its use. Frankincense is still harvested from the trees in Dhofar but is mostly used by local people now.

The colorful history of the region includes a period of rule at the beginning of the 1800s by an eccentric and strangely enlightened former buccaneer and slave-trader named Muhammad bin Aqil Ajaibi. He was assassinated in 1829, however, and the sultan reasserted his authority by sending troops. After that time, Dhofar has been consistently ruled from Muscat.

Salalah, like most of Oman's once-glorious shipping ports, maintains just a fraction of its former influence. But the ancient city is staging a comeback. In 2001, the city beat Hong Kong and Singapore to the title of the world's most efficient container port. The $400 million public-private partnership that operates the port served to underscore Muscat's commitment to position the country as a modern, high-tech player in the global shipping business.

The rural people of Dhofar are farmers, and the mountain people are herdsmen who love their animals—cattle, goats, and sheep. The coastal people have intermarried with the East Africans who have come to inhabit the area, and the culture shows the African influence through its lively music, its food, and its colorful dress.

CELEBRATIONS

Besides the splendid wedding parties that form the basis for community celebrations throughout Oman, the biggest holidays in the country revolve around two important Islamic festivals.

Eid al-Fitr (the Feast of Fast Breaking) falls at the end of the Ramadan observance. This festival is a time of great rejoicing, with song and dance, feasting and visiting with family and friends. The men entertain the crowds with breathtaking sword dances, and the sounds of music and gun salutes fill the air.

The Eid al-Adha (the Feast of Sacrifice) is a more serious occasion. It takes place at the end of the period when Muslims are supposed to make their way to Mecca on pilgrimage. Eid al-Adha commemorates the willingness to the patriarch Abraham (Ibrahim) to sacrifice his son to God. Instead, God provided a sheep, so traditionally Muslim families would slaughter and eat a sheep on this day.

National Day, scheduled around the Sultan's birthday, is marked with big parades and festivities in a public display of national pride.

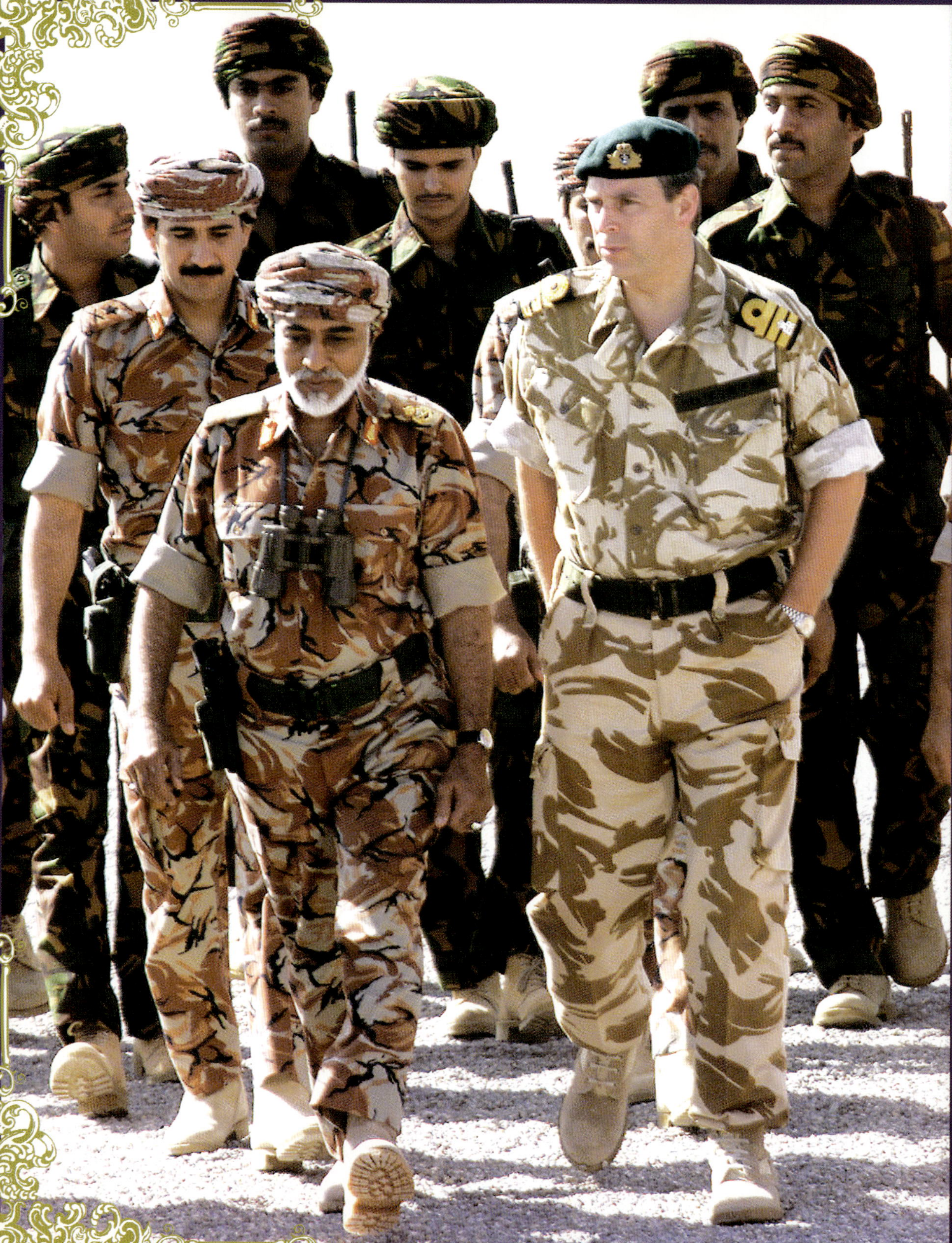

Sultan Qaboos walks with Prince Andrew of Great Britain (right) before watching a joint British-Omani military exercise, *Saif Sareea II* (Swift Sword II), in October 2001. Since the 1970s Oman has been a key logistics and intelligence center for U.S. and British operations in the Persian Gulf and Indian Ocean.

Foreign Relations

Despite its tiny size, its moderate oil reserves, and its relatively small population, Oman has been a key player in Middle Eastern affairs. For one thing, there's its location on the strategically critical Strait of Hormuz; for another, there's the considerable skill that Sultan Qaboos has exercised as a peacemaker.

The northernmost tip of Oman, the Musandam Peninsula, creates a narrow chokepoint between the Sea of Oman and the Arabian Gulf (or Persian Gulf—depending on which side of the highly contested sea one lives on, the title is a matter of great debate). About half of the known oil reserves in the world are located in the gulf region, and there have been times when 70 percent of the world's oil supplies have passed through the strait. The traffic lanes used by the oil tankers are on the Omani side of the gulf, so Oman is responsible for the safety of a very large part of the world's oil commerce.

In a region noted for bitter rivalries and explosive tensions, Oman's consistently moderate and pragmatic approach has made it a leader in efforts to keep the peace in the Middle East. Sultan Qaboos's quiet, behind-the-scenes diplomacy has helped his neighbors resolve conflicts time after time, and he has worked hard to keep strong ties with all the countries in the region. Even at the height of the Iran-Iraq war, Oman maintained diplomatic relations with both countries—a remarkable feat, considering the extreme hostility that each side held toward the other.

Oman has been a consistent friend to the United States, and even more closely allied with Great Britain, since the early 1800s. It has served as an island of stability in troubled times, which is why the U.S. sought an arrangement to use its lands for military training and to keep stores of weapons there so that it could meet aggression in the area with a rapid response. Oman played a key role in the Gulf War in 1991 and again during the U.S. strike in Afghanistan in the fall of 2001.

Consistent with Omani tradition, however, Qaboos is a strongly independent thinker, and his administration has differed with the United States, Iran, and Iraq on matters of principle. And Omani citizens, while generally sympathetic to the West, are far from unquestioning in their support of U.S. military action in the region.

IRAN AND IRAQ

In 1979, Iranian revolutionaries toppled the U.S.-supported shah of Iran and began more than a decade of turmoil. The charismatic Muslim fundamentalist Ayatollah Ruholla Khomeini took the helm of the country. Khomeini called the United States "the Great Satan" and ordered his followers to resist influence from the West.

Oman's response has been notably different from that of the United States, which isolated Iran and imposed sanctions. Oman shares the gulf and the Strait of Hormuz with Iran. With its 66 mil-

FOREIGN RELATIONS

In January 1979 Muslim fundamentalists—disciples of the exiled Ayatollah Ruholla Khomeini (1902–1989), a Shiite cleric—overthrew the U.S.-supported government of the Shah of Iran. Khomeini returned to Iran in triumph, and soon instituted a new government under Islamic law. The Ayatollah attempted to "export" his revolution to neighboring countries, such as Oman, but the radical movement failed to take hold outside of Iran.

lion people and a vast arsenal at its disposal, Iran is a serious force to be reckoned with, and Oman prefers to try to resolve problems through dialog rather than by trying to isolate the Persian giant.

Iran hasn't always made it easy. Under the shah, relations were friendly, with the shah supporting Oman during its war with Islamic rebels in Dhofar. But after the Iranian Revolution, the relationship grew tense. Khomeini disapproved of Oman's ties with the U.S. and Great Britain. He supported attempts to export his revolution through radical Islamic movements in Oman and other neighboring countries.

Even after Khomeini's death, Iran's expansionist behaviors continued. In 1993, Tehran announced that it was taking control of Omani waters in the Strait of Hormuz. Making matters worse, Iran bought military submarines and positioned Silkworm missiles overlooking the strait. Oman responded with a military buildup on

Saddam Hussein became president of Iraq in 1979—the same year Khomeini's supporters overthrew the Shah of Iran and instituted a fundamentalist regime. However, Iraq, an Arab nation with a Sunni Muslim ruling class, was soon at odds with Iran and its Shiite government. The two nations fought a bitter war from 1980 to 1988. Oman maintained domestic relations with both countries during the war, but also made preparations in case either Iran or Iraq set their sights on Omani territory. In addition to improving Oman's military, Sultan Qaboos facilitated the formation of the Gulf Cooperation Council, an alliance of the Gulf States, in 1981.

the Musandam Peninsula and increased patrols, but maintained diplomatic relations.

Oman sees Iran's importance as a counterbalance to Iraq, which has engaged in several aggressive attempts to take over lands belonging to its neighbors since the late 1970s—most famously in Kuwait, which led to the Persian Gulf War in 1991. Oman has maintained diplomatic relations with Iraq since 1976, but as with Iran these relations have frequently been uneasy.

Led by Saddam Hussein and the Arab nationalist Ba'ath Party, Iraq is as anti-West as its bitter enemy, Iran. Angered by Oman's reliance on British military assistance during the rebellion in Dhofar, Iraq opposed Oman's admission into the Arab League in 1971. Even worse, Iraq trained and sheltered the Dhofar rebels and provided a sanctuary to the Popular Front for the Liberation of Oman until 1975. When the Dhofar war ended in 1976, Oman and Iraq decided to put the past behind them and establish diplomatic relations.

INTERNATIONAL PEACEMAKER

During the late 1970s Qaboos broke ranks with most of his Arab League colleagues by supporting Egyptian President Anwar Sadat's historic visit to Israel in November 1977 and his role in the Camp David peace accords in September 1978. He was one of only three Arab leaders to do so. "Despite all of the difficulties, Camp David has brought the solutions to the Middle East problems closer," Qaboos told *Newsweek* reporter Chris Harper in a 1980 interview. "Up to now, no one has come up with a better approach."

Arab response to Egypt was swift and sharp. Egypt was voted out of the Arab League, and the group cut its diplomatic relations with Sadat. But Qaboos went on to earn a level of respect from Arab leaders that transcended their differing views.

Following the Dhofar war, Qaboos led an effort to pull the Arab states together in a coalition that would cooperate to fight threats to the region. It was Sultan Qaboos who invited the Gulf States to a November 1976 meeting in Muscat, in order to discuss the potential of a strategic alliance among the neighboring countries. At that first meeting, the countries were extremely reluctant to cooperate, and many observers did not think it would be possible to get the fractious states of the Middle East to cooperate on anything as potentially controversial as defense. The Gulf States rejected several of Qaboos's attempts to pull the countries of the region together for mutual defense.

In 1979, when radical Islamic fundamentalists led by the Ayatollah Khomeini deposed the shah of Iran, Qaboos called on his neighbors to join in an effort to prevent aggression by the radicals. He proposed that the gulf countries cooperate in a $100 million protection plan for the Strait of Hormuz. But the Gulf States dismissed the idea once again.

Frustrated with the inaction of the Gulf States, Qaboos went to the United States with a plan. The visit ended in the 1980 Facilities Access Agreement, which gave the U.S. military access to Omani bases under specified conditions—one of which was advance notice of military activity from those bases. The U.S. could keep supplies and fuel in Oman for quick access in an emergency, and they could also use the major air base on Masirah Island.

The United States was quick to take advantage of the facilities agreement, using Masirah as a base when they tried to rescue 52 Americans held hostage inside the U.S. Embassy in Iran by Khomeini's supporters. Equipment problems caused the April 1980 mission to be aborted before the rescue force could enter Iran. When Omanis learned of the failed rescue attempt, many felt betrayed and angry because they had not been notified about the mission in advance, and their government had not had an opportunity to disagree. Many Omanis felt their country had been tricked into lending its support to a military operation against Iran.

The U.S. Facilities Access Agreement helped Oman feel a bit more secure in the short run, but it didn't help the country's relations with its neighbors, and it definitely didn't remove the need for cooperation among the gulf countries. When the Iran-Iraq War broke out in 1980, the need for cooperation became undeniable, and the other leaders came around to Qaboos's way of thinking. He held a preparatory meeting in Muscat, prior to the formal founding

Foreign Relations

U.S. President Jimmy Carter listens to Israeli Prime Minister Menachem Begin (left) and Egyptian President Anwar Sadat (right) during a meeting at Camp David, the presidential retreat in Maryland, in September 1978. The Camp David accords, and the Egypt-Israel peace treaty signed the next year, were angrily denounced by many in the Arab world. Oman's Sultan Qaboos was one of the few Arab leaders to support Sadat. The sultan's willingness to go against popular opinion and support policies that are fair has made him a statesman respected both in the West and throughout the Arab world.

of the GCC in May 1981 in Abu Dhabi. Oman advocated that the GCC link cooperation on social, economic, and political matters as well as military ones. And an Omani was appointed to one of the highest positions: assistant secretary-general for political affairs.

By the mid-1980s, Qaboos had earned the respect of western leaders and was recognized as a force for stability in the region. The relationship between Oman and the West was military and strategic as well as economic. In 1986 the desert plains of Dhofar became the staging ground for one of the biggest military training exercises

In the spring of 2002, U.S. Vice President Dick Cheney toured the Middle East, meeting with Arab leaders to line up support in the region for an attack on Iraq intended to depose Saddam Hussein. Although Oman supported the first phase of the U.S.-led war on terrorism, Sultan Qaboos initially expressed his opposition to war with Iraq.

in Great Britain's history, a mock battlefield known as *Saif Sareea*, or "Swift Sword." Oman became a key player during the Gulf War of 1991, in which a coalition of western and Arab nations fought Iraq to liberate Kuwait, the small Arab country Saddam Hussein's forces had invaded the previous summer. Before and during the conflict, U.S. troops kept supplies in Oman and used Masirah Island as a staging area for their attacks.

At the same time, Qaboos reaffirmed his ties to both Kuwait and Iraq and tried to serve as a mediator between the two countries. After the war, when the United States decided to impose sanctions on Iraq, Oman refused to follow suit, preferring to try to influence the country through diplomatic relations.

More recently, in the U.S.-led war on terrorism Oman has once again played a role. In the aftermath of the September 11, 2001, attacks on the World Trade Center and the Pentagon, Oman offered its facilities and lands to help the Western powers prepare for a strike on Afghanistan, where the suspected mastermind of the attacks, Osama bin Laden, was believed to be hiding. In the fall of 2001, more than 20,000 British soldiers came to Oman and participated in Swift Sword II, a training exercise preparing them to fight in Afghanistan. However, when the United States began talk of expanding its war into other Middle Eastern countries where bin Laden's al-Qaeda terrorist network might be hiding (particularly Iraq), Oman joined with the other Arab nations in speaking out against such an offensive.

During the summer and fall of 2002, as U.S. leaders discussed the possibility of an attack on Iraq, Omani Foreign Minister Yousuf bin Alawi bin Abdullah declared Oman's opposition to U.S. action against Iraq or any Muslim country. Any military action in the Middle East should be resolved under the auspices of the United Nations, he said.

Defense spending in Oman

For all his talk of peace, however, Sultan Qaboos has invested billions of dollars in preparing for war. His administration has been marked by a mounting stockpile of high-tech weaponry, from F-16 fighter jets to Superlynx helicopters. A World Bank study warned that the country was heading for serious economic problems because of its high level of military spending, particularly given its declining revenues from oil. In 1997, a ranking of countries according to the percentage of their economies dedicated to the military put Oman near the top of the list of countries not at war, with 15.3

percent of its budget per year devoted to defense. That level put the country on the top 10 list—ahead even of Saudi Arabia, one of the world's biggest military spenders, and on a par with Iraq, which was still under ongoing air attacks and economic sanctions by the United States.

Oman's high level of military spending, along with the resulting drain on its economy, is right in line with most of its Arab neighbors. The Arab Monetary Fund reported that between 1990 and 2000, Oman, the United Arab Emirates, Saudi Arabia, Bahrain, Kuwait, and Qatar allocated between 26 and 30 percent of their total expenditures to the defense sector, adding up to more than $240 billion—more than a third of their total revenues during that period. After the report was released, the *Financial Times of London* echoed the earlier warnings of the World Bank, saying the countries face a bleak future with a sluggish economy and low spending on social reforms and employment initiatives.

Good neighbor policies

Oman has also been in the forefront in strengthening ties between the Arab countries and their neighbors along the Indian Ocean rim. In 1997 it was one of the seven founding members of the Indian Ocean Rim Association, an organization that sought to strengthen trading partnerships and cooperative investments within the region. The original countries, besides Oman, included India, Australia, South Africa, Singapore, Kenya, and Mauritius. The association now includes 19 members, including numerous countries in Africa, Southeast Asia, and the Arabian Peninsula.

The historic ties between India and Oman were highlighted in 1997 with Sultan Qaboos's official state visit to New Delhi, which was followed the next year with a visit to Muscat by Indian Prime Minister Atal Behari Vajpayee. Other official Omani delegations have met with officials in Sri Lanka, Japan, China, and Brunei.

Closer to home, Oman concentrated on mending fences with its neighbors. In 1990, after centuries of border rivalries and conflicts, Oman and Saudi Arabia finally settled on a mutually agreeable border; in 1992, the new maps showing this border were officially signed in a ceremony in Riyadh. In 1995, another long-running border rivalry came to an end when Oman and Yemen finally demarcated their borders. And in 1997, work began on a 151-mile-long (243-km-long) highway, funded by Oman, that would link the Dhofar province with cities inside Yemen.

CHRONOLOGY

c. 3000 B.C.: Significant settlements are established in the Buraimi Oasis area, as well as the Dhofar region.

c. 2000 B.C.: Copper is discovered in the Sohar area along the Batinah Coast in the north, and an empire known as Magan grows around the mining and trade of copper.

c. A.D. 300: The city of Ubar, a major trading center for frankincense, is destroyed.

570: The Prophet Muhammad is born in the city of Mecca; within 80 years, all the people of Oman will be converted to Islam.

751: Election of first imam in Oman.

971: Sohar sacked and destroyed by the Buyids.

1153: Maliks of the Nabhan take over Oman and depose the Imams.

1435: Imam rule restored.

1507: The Portuguese invade Oman.

1587: Construction begins on two forts (Jalali and Miran) built by Portuguese in Muscat.

1624: Nasir bin Murshid elected; first Imam of the Yaruba dynasty.

1646: Trade begins with British East India Company.

1650: Sultan bin Saif al-Ya'aribi drives the Portuguese out of Muscat.

1718: Civil war begins in Oman.

1738: Persians invade Oman and rule the country.

1744: Persians driven out of Oman; Ahmad bin Said becomes Imam.

1800: Wahhabis capture Buraimi; around this time Muhammad bin Aqil Ajaibi assumes power in Dhofar.

1804: Reign of Sultan Sayyid Said bin Sultan begins.

1913: Taimur bin Faisal begins reign.

1920: The Treaty of Sib is signed; it becomes the ruling document of the country for the next 35 years.

1932: Said bin Taimur becomes ruler of Oman.

1955: Omanis regain control of Buraimi from Saudis, who had occupied it since 1952.

CHRONOLOGY

1965: The Dhofar Liberation Front begins fighting for an independent Dhofar; the rebellion will continue until 1975.

1967: Oil production begins in Oman.

1970: Qaboos bin Said becomes the sultan of Oman.

1971: Oman joins the United Nations and the Arab League.

1979: Peace agreement brokered at Camp David between Egypt and Israel is signed; Ayatollah Khomeini assumes power in Iran.

1980: Facilities Access Agreement with U.S. signed; Iran-Iraq War begins.

1981: Gulf Cooperation Council founded.

1990: Majlis al-Shura created; Iraq invades Kuwait.

1991: Oman and other Arab countries participate in the Gulf War, driving Iraqi forces out of Kuwait; Madrid Peace Conference held to create a framework for peace in the Middle East.

1993: Oman becomes involved in a standoff with Iran over the waters around the Strait of Hormuz.

1996: A constitution, called the Basic Law, is passed.

1997: Oman becomes a founding member of the Indian Ocean Rim Association.

2000: Oman joins the World Trade Organization.

2001: Oman opens world's most efficient container port in Salalah; Sultan Qaboos meets with Egyptian president Hosni Mubarak to discuss the Israeli-Palestinian situation in the Middle East.

2002: Oman opposes military action against Iraq unless it is carried out under the auspices of the United Nations.

2003: The Arab League meets in Bahrain.

GLOSSARY

abdicate—to formally or officially give up a high government office.

alluvial plain—an area where the soil is made up of silt, gravel, sand, clay, or other material once deposited by running water.

burkha—face covering worn by some Muslim women.

caliph—a Muslim ruler who asserts divine or religious authority to rule.

coup—the sudden overthrow of a government and seizure of political power.

depose—to remove somebody from a position of power.

dishdasha—robe worn by men; usually white, but sometimes light blue.

djinn—in Arabian folklore, a spirit with supernatural powers (also called a genie or jinni).

falaj—a canal system used to irrigate crops.

fjord—a long, narrow coastal inlet with steep sides.

gross domestic product (GDP)—the total value of all goods and services produced within a country in a year.

halwa—candy made of *ghee* (a type of butter), brown sugar, and ground almonds.

Ibadi Islam—a type of Islam practiced by most Omanis that developed during the 8th century.

imam—a spiritual leader of the Muslim people. In Oman, imams have also been political and, at times, military leaders.

infidel—to a Muslim, someone who does not follow the Islamic faith.

Islamist—espousing radically fundamentalist Islamic doctrine that is usually hostile to Western societies and ideas.

khanjar—a curved dagger.

kohl—eyeliner.

majlis—a traditional council session with a leader.

oases—isolated fertile areas surrounding water sources in a desert.

pension—a fixed sum of money paid regularly as compensation or reward.

people of 'Ad—the ancient people of the Dhofar Mountains who first harvested and traded frankincense.

GLOSSARY

privitization—to change control of a business or industry from public to private.

rial—unit of money used in Oman.

spice—aromatic plant substances, such as nutmeg, ginger, or pepper, used as flavorings; these were prized, and hard to get, in Europe during the Middle Ages.

subsidy—a monetary gift in order to help pay expenses.

sultan—the title of a sovereign ruler in a Muslim country.

tahr—a type of mountain goat that was once nearly extinct in Oman.

trade wind—a prevailing tropical wind that blows toward the equator.

wadi—a dry riverbed that fills with water during the rainy season.

Wahhabi Islam—a movement to reform Islam, founded in the 18th century by Muhammad ibn Abd al-Wahab. Wahhabism is a conservative, fundamentalist movement; it calls for strict observance of the Qur'an in all aspects of Muslim life.

wali—a regional governor.

FURTHER READING

Allen, Calvin, and Rigsbee, W. Lynn. *Oman Under Qaboos: From Coup to Constitution, 1970–1996*. London: Frank Cass, 2000.

Bulloch, John. *The Persian Gulf Unveiled*. New York: Congdon and Weed, 1984.

Darlow, Michael, and Fawkes, Richard. *The Last Corner of Arabia*. London: Namara Publications and Quartet Books, 1976.

Hawley, Sir Donald. *Oman and Its Renaissance*. London: Stacey International, 1977.

Joyce, Miriam. *The Sultanate of Oman: A Twentieth-Century History*. Westport, Conn.: Praeger Publishers, 2001.

Miller, Judith. "Creating Modern Oman: An Interview with Sultan Qaboos." *Foreign Affairs*, May/June 1997.

Morris, James. *Sultan of Oman*. London: Faber and Faber, 1957.

Owtram, Francis. *A Modern History of Oman*. London: I.B. Tavris, 2002.

Porter, J.D., ed. *Oman and the Persian Gulf, 1835–1949*. Salisbury, N.C.: Documentary Publications, 1982.

Riphenburg, Carol J. *Oman: Political Development in a Changing World*. Westport, Conn.: Praeger Publishers, 1998.

Wikan, Unni. *Behind the Veil in Arabia: Women in Oman*. Baltimore: Johns Hopkins University Press, 1982.

Wingate, Ronald. *Not in the Limelight*. London: Hutchinsons and Co., 1959.

INTERNET RESOURCES

http://www.oman.org/

The website of the Oman Studies Centre provides information and links on Oman.

http://www.geocities.com/suonnoch/Oman/Omanindx.html

The Off-Road in Oman site captures much of the natural beauty of Oman and includes valuable tips for travelers.

http://www.newsbriefsoman.info/

Oman Newsbriefs has a wealth of links to all the relevant newspapers in Oman and in the region, a compendium of regional businesses and government sites, and organizations active in Oman.

http://www.omanforum.com/

A collection of discussion groups on everything from festivals to public spitting in Oman

http://www.omanet.com/

The official site of the Sultanate of Oman, complete with waving flag and national anthem, minister's message, links to all government ministries and committees, tourism facts, and business information.

http://www.ociped.com/

The site for the Oman Centre for Investment Promotion and Economic Development.

http://www.mctmnet.gov.om/

This site includes information about the history and politics of Muscat, Oman's capital city, as well as a discussion forum, directorates, and services.

http://www.moneoman.gov.om/

The Oman Ministry of National Economy is a good source for general socioeconomic information about Oman.

http://www.omannews.com/

The Oman News Agency.

INDEX

bin Abdullah, Yousuf bin Alawi, 107
Abu Bakr, 73
Abu Dhabi, 24, 50–51
'Ad, people of, 34–35
Afghanistan, 100, 107
agriculture, 14–15, 22, 24–25, 65, *66*, 70–71, 85–86, 96
Al Akhdar Mountains, *85*
Al bu Said dynasty, 40–47, 49, 63, 75, 91–92
Albuquerque, Alfonso de, *39*
Alexander the Great, 35
Alsalmy, Abdulla bin Hamid (Noor A'Dein), 45
Andrew, Prince, *99*
bin Aqil Ajaibi, Muhammad, 96
Arab League, 103
Arabian Gulf (Persian Gulf), 99
Arabian horses, *78*
architecture, 84–85
artisanship, 83–84, *86*
Authority for the Settlement of Commercial Disputes (ASCD), 64
   See also judicial system
Ayatollah Khomeini. See Khomeini, Ayatollah Ruholla

Bahlah, 94
Bahrain, 40, *106*
Baluchis, 78
Barka, 91–93
Basic Law (constitution), 63
   See also government
Batinah Coast, 19, 20, *21*, 22–23, 34, 78, *80*, 85, 89, 90–93
Bedouin tribes, 24, 79, *80*, 86–87, 89–90
Begin, Menachem, *105*
bin Laden, Osama, 107
bin Said, Sultan Qaboos. See Qaboos bin Said (Sultan)
Brunei, 58
Bukha, 27
Bulloch, John, 52, 86
Buraimi dispute, *50*, 51–52
Buraimi Oasis, 23–24

Camp David Accords, 55, *105*
Carter, Jimmy, *105*
Central Oman, 24
   See also Oman, regions of
Cheney, Dick, *109*
Christianity, 35, 75, 96
chronology (of Oman), 110–111

climate, 19–21, *23*, 95
Consultative Council (Majlis al-Shura), 58, 60–63
   See also government; Majlis al-Dawla
copper, 34, 37
Council of Minsiters, 58
   See also government
currency, *66*

dates, 22, 45, 86
debt, 49
defense spending, in Oman, 107–108
Dhofar Liberation Front, 53
Dhofar region, *19*, 20–21, 24–25, 34, *35*, *80*
   cities in, 95–96
   civil war in, 53, 55, 58, 101, 103
dhows, *33*, 36, *37*, 93
   See also sea trade

economy, 65–71, 107–108
education, 14, *15*, 50, 58, 59, 66, 82
Egypt, 103, *105*
Eid al-Adha, 97
   See also Islam
Eid al-Fitr, 97
   See also Islam
environmental issues, 16–17, 27, 67–68

Facilities Access Agreement (1980), 104
bin Faisal, Sultan Taimur, 43, 45–47, *48*, 49, 91
   See also Al bu Said dynasty
falaj (irrigation system), 19, 22, *70*, 71, 86
Fatimah, 72–73
   See also Islam
festivals, Islamic, 97
fishing, *68*, 85
France, 44
frankincense, *19*, 24–25, 29, *30*, 34–35, 37, 95–96

Gama, Vasco da, 39
gender roles. See women
government, 16, 47, 58–63
Great Britain, 24, 85–86
   relationship of, with Oman, 40, 42–47, 49, 51–52, *53*, 55, *99*, 100, 105
Green Mountain (Jabal al-Akhdar), 23
Gulf Cooperation Council (GCC), 55, *102*, 103, 105, *106*
Gulf War, 100, 102, 105–106

Hajar Mountains, 20, *21*, 22–23, 26
halwa, *84*, 94

Numbers in **bold italic** refer to captions.

INDEX

Hamasa, 52
Hazam, **48**
Hinduism, 75
Hosman, Elizabeth, **48**, 93
Hussein, Saddam, **102**, 103, 106, **109**

ibn Ibad, Abd Allah, 74
Ibadi Islam, 14, 16, 47, 60, 64, 74–75
    See also Islam
Imam Wars, 93
imams, 16, 41, 42–43, 45, 46–47, 74–75
    See also Islam
Incense Coast. See Dhofar region
India, 108
Indian Ocean, **33**, 36, 39
Indian Ocean Rim Association, 108
Inner Oman, 24, 93–94
    See also Oman, regions of
Iran, 100–102
    hostages in, 104
Iran-Iraq war, 16, 104
Iraq, 102–103, 106, 107–108, **109**
Islam, 14, 16, 36–37, **48**, **77**, 78–79, **101**, 104
    festivals of, 97
    Five Pillars of, 72
    Shiite and Sunni divisions in, 72–75
Islamic law (Sharia), 44–45, 63–65
    See also Islam

Jabal al-Akhdar (Green Mountain), 23
Jabal Qamar (mountains), 24
Jabal Samhan (mountains), 24
Johnson, Eric, 52
judicial system, 63–65

Khan, Ehtisham-Ud-Dowlah, 46–47
    See also Wingate, Ronald
Khariji, 74
    See also Ibadi Islam
Khasab, 27
Khomeini, Ayatollah Ruholla, 100–101, 104
Koran. See Qur'an
Kumzar, 27
Kuwait, 60, 102, **106**

Lawrence, T.E. (Lawrence of Arabia), **30**
Limah, 27
literacy rate, 58
    See also education

Magan Empire, 34
Majlis al-Dawla, 62
    See also government

Majlis al-Shura. See Consultative Council (Majlis al-Shura)
Marco Polo, **38**, 39
Masirah Island, 24, 104, 106
Mecca, 36, 72, 97
    See also Islam
Miller, Judith, 63
Ministry of Water Resources, 71
    See also government; water resources
Mirani, 90
missionaries, **48**
Morris, James, 51–52
Moscha, **35**
Muhammad, 36, 47, 72
    See also Islam
Musandam Peninsula (Ras al-Jibal), 26–27, 99
Muscat, 19, 20–21, 22, **39**, 40, 41, 42–43, **48**, 89, 90, **95**
Muscat Securities Market, **67**
Muttrah, 40, 41, 90, **91**

National Day, 97
natural resources, **66**
Nizwa, 23, **41**, 93–94

oil, 14, **15**, 17, 24, 50–53, 54, **57**, 58, 65, **66**, 67, **69**, 99, **106**
    and environmental issues, 67–68
Oman
    chronology, 110–111
    cities, 89–97
    climate, 19–21, **23**, 95
    conquest of, by Portugal, 39–40
    culture, 83–87, 97
    defense spending, 107–108
    division of, until 1970, 42
    economy, 65–71, 107–108
    education, 14, **15**, 50, 58, 59, 66, 82
    environmental issues, 16–17, 27–29
    foreign relations, 16, 55, 99–109
    geographic features of, 20, **23**, **25**
    government, 16, 47, 58–63
    and Great Britain, 40, 42–47, 49, 51–52, **53**, 55, 85–86, **99**, 100, 105
    gross domestic product (GDP) of, 65, **66**
    judicial system, 63–65
    population, 20, 78, **79**, **80**, 86–87, 89
    rainfall, 19, 21, 24
    regions of, 21–27, 89–97
    ruling dynasties of, 40–47, 49–50
    and the United States of America, 41, 55, 100, 104, 106–107
    water resources, 17, 70–71, 86

INDEX

oryx, Arabian, 27–29
   See also wildlife
Osama bin Laden, 107
Ottoman Empire, 39

people of 'Ad, 34–35
Persian Empire, 40–41, 92–93
Persian Gulf (Arabian Gulf), 99
Phoenicians, 93
Popular Front for the Liberation of Oman, 103
Portugal, 39–40, 94

Qaboos bin Said (Sultan), 14, **15**, 16, 42, 53–55, 75, **92,** 95, **99**
   and the economy, 65–71
   and environmental issues, 27–29
   foreign relations skills of, 99–100, **102**, 103–108
   and political reform, 58–63
   and women's rights, 81–82
   See also Al bu Said dynasty
Qalhat, 40
bin al Qassim, Abu Ubaida bin Abdulla, 36
   See also sea trade
Qatar, **106**
Qur'an, 16, **30**, 60, 72
   See also Islam
Qurayyat, **89**

rainfall, 19, 21, 24
Ramadan, 97
   See also Islam
Ras al-Hadd, 29
Ras al-Jibal (Musandam Peninsula), 26–27
Riyam beach, **28**
Rub' al Khali desert, 13, 20, 24, **30**, 33
Rustaq, 23, 44, 94
Ruwi, **92**

Sadat, Anwar, 103, **105**
bin Said, Ahmad, 41, 75, 91–92, 95
   See also Al bu Said dynasty
bin Said, Sultan Qaboos. See Qaboos bin Said (Sultan)
bin Saif al-Ya'aribi, 40
ibn Saif I, 40
ibn Saif II, 40
Salalah, 25, 53, 67, 89, 95–96
bin Saleh, Isa, 45
Saudi Arabia, 20, 33, 47, 51–52, **57**, 60, 82, **106**, 109
Sea of Oman, 99
sea trade, **33**, 36–37, 96
Sharia (Islamic law), 44–45, 63–65
   See also Islam
Shi'a Muslims. See Islam
Sib, 46, 91
Sinbad the Sailor, 13, **37**, 90
   See also sea trade
Sohar, 34, 36, 40, 41, 44, 80, 90–92
Soviet Union, 55
Storm, Harold, **48**
Strait of Hormuz, 14, 26, 99, 100–102, 104
bin Sultan, Sayyid Said, 41–42
   See also Al bu Said dynasty
Sultan Qaboos bin Said. See Qaboos bin Said (Sultan)
Sultan Qaboos Grand Mosque, **73**
Sumhuram, **35**
Sunni Muslims. See Islam
Sur, **37**, 43, 44, 93
Suwaiq, **37**, **48**, 93
Swahili, 37

bin Taimur, Said, 49–54, 95
   See also Al bu Said dynasty
Tales of the Arabian Nights, 13, **30**, **37**
Thesiger, Wilfred, 93–94
Thomas, Bertram, 49, 94
tourism, 68
   See also economy
trade
   ancient, 24–26, **33**, 34–35, 39, **77,** 78, 95–96
   arms, 42, 44–45
   sea, **33**, 36–37, 96
   slave, 37, 39, 40, 42, 45
Treaty of Sib, 47, 49
Trucial Oman Levies, 52
   See also Buraimi dispute
bin Turki, Sultan Faisal, 42–45
   See also Al bu Said dynasty

Ubar, 13, 26, **30–31**, 34–35, 96
unemployment, 65–66
United Arab Emirates (UAE), 26, 50, **57**, 82, **106**
United Nations, **50**
United States of America, 16, 24, 41, 55, 82, 100, 104, 106–107

Vajpayee, Atal Behari, 108

Wadi Sama'il, 23
wadis (oases), 22, 23
Wahhabis, 47, 51
Wahiba Sands, 24
water resources, 17, 70–71, 86
Wikan, Unni, 79–80

INDEX

wildlife, 15, 27–29
Wingate, Ronald, 46–47, 49, 91
    See also Great Britain
women
    customs of, in Oman, 78–80
    role of, in society, 15, 16, 61, **62**, 81–82
World Trade Organization (WTO), 67

al-Ya'aribi, Imam bin Saif, 94
al-Ya'aribi, Nassir bin Murshid, 40
Ya'aribi dynasty, 40
Yemen, 53, **54**, 55, 82, 109

Zafar, 25–26
Zanzibar, 40, 41, 78

PICTURE CREDITS

2:	© OTTN Publishing
3:	Yann Arthus-Bertrand/Corbis
12:	Bojan Brecelj/Corbis
15:	Courtesy of the Embassy of the Sultanate of Oman
18:	Arthur Thévenart/Corbis
21:	© OTTN Publishing
22:	Courtesy of the Embassy of the Sultanate of Oman
25:	Courtesy of the Embassy of the Sultanate of Oman
26:	Courtesy of the Embassy of the Sultanate of Oman
28:	Courtesy of the Embassy of the Sultanate of Oman
31:	Courtesy National Aeronautics and Space Administration
32:	Bibliotheque Nationale, Paris
35:	Dave G. Houser/Houserstock
37:	Courtesy of the Embassy of the Sultanate of Oman
38:	Bibliotheque Nationale, Paris
39:	Hulton/Archive/Getty Images
41:	Courtesy of the Embassy of the Sultanate of Oman
43:	Arne Hodalic/Corbis
50:	Bettmann/Corbis
53:	Hulton/Archive/Getty Images
54:	Courtesy of the Embassy of the Sultanate of Oman
56:	David Forman; Eye Ubiquitous/Corbis
59:	© OTTN Publishing
61:	Courtesy of the Embassy of the Sultanate of Oman
62:	Courtesy of the Embassy of the Sultanate of Oman
67:	Courtesy of the Embassy of the Sultanate of Oman
68:	Jon Hicks/Corbis
69:	both Courtesy of the Embassy of the Sultanate of Oman
70:	both Courtesy of the Embassy of the Sultanate of Oman
73:	Courtesy of the Embassy of the Sultanate of Oman
76:	Courtesy of the Embassy of the Sultanate of Oman
78:	Courtesy of the Embassy of the Sultanate of Oman
80:	© OTTN Publishing
81:	Dave G. Houser/Houserstock
82:	Dave G. Houser/Houserstock
83:	Getty Images
84:	both Courtesy of the Embassy of the Sultanate of Oman
85:	Arne Hodalic/Corbis
86:	both Courtesy of the Embassy of the Sultanate of Oman
88:	Arthur Thévenart/Corbis
91:	Courtesy of the Embassy of the Sultanate of Oman
92:	Courtesy of the Embassy of the Sultanate of Oman
95:	Courtesy of the Embassy of the Sultanate of Oman
98:	Reuters NewMedia Inc./Corbis
101:	Hulton/Archive/Getty Images
102:	INA/Getty Images
105:	Jimmy Carter Library
106:	AFP/Corbis

Cover photos: (front) PictureQuest; (back) Courtesy of the Embassy of the Sultanate of Oman

CONTRIBUTORS

The **FOREIGN POLICY RESEARCH INSTITUTE (FPRI)** served as editorial consultants for the MODERN MIDDLE EAST NATIONS series. FPRI is one of the nation's oldest "think tanks." The Institute's Middle East Program focuses on Gulf security, monitors the Arab-Israeli peace process, and sponsors an annual conference for teachers on the Middle East, plus periodic briefings on key developments in the region.

Among the FPRI's trustees is a former Secretary of State and a former Secretary of the Navy (and among the FPRI's former trustees and interns, two current Undersecretaries of Defense), not to mention two university presidents emeritus, a foundation president, and several active or retired corporate CEOs.

The scholars of FPRI include a former aide to three U.S. Secretaries of State, a Pulitzer Prize–winning historian, a former president of Swarthmore College and a Bancroft Prize–winning historian, and two former staff members of the National Security Council. And the FPRI counts among its extended network of scholars—especially its Inter-University Study Groups—representatives of diverse disciplines, including political science, history, economics, law, management, religion, sociology, and psychology.

DR. HARVEY SICHERMAN is president and director of the Foreign Policy Research Institute in Philadelphia, Pennsylvania. He has extensive experience in writing, research, and analysis of U.S. foreign and national security policy, both in government and out. He served as Special Assistant to Secretary of State Alexander M. Haig Jr. and as a member of the Policy Planning Staff of Secretary of State James A. Baker III. Dr. Sicherman was also a consultant to Secretary of the Navy John F. Lehman Jr. (1982–1987) and Secretary of State George Shultz (1988).

A graduate of the University of Scranton (B.S., History, 1966), Dr. Sicherman earned his Ph.D. at the University of Pennsylvania (Political Science, 1971), where he received a Salvatori Fellowship. He is author or editor of numerous books and articles, including *America the Vulnerable: Our Military Problems and How to Fix Them* (FPRI, 2002) and *Palestinian Autonomy, Self-Government and Peace* (Westview Press, 1993). He edits *Peacefacts*, an FPRI bulletin that monitors the Arab-Israeli peace process.

TRACY L. BARNETT is a freelance journalist and the author of several books. She has taught writing and editing at the University of Missouri School of Journalism, and is the founding editor of *Adelante*, a bilingual Spanish-English community newspaper in Missouri. Her great passion is travel; she has been to a dozen countries, but she wants to see them all before she dies. She is translating a collection of Venezuelan stories for children and is working with a Peruvian author on a collection of stories about the Quechua people.